Teresa Southwick lives with her husband in Las Vegas, the city that reinvents itself every day. An avid fan of romance novels, she is delighted to be living out her dream of writing for Mills & Boon.

D1740374

Also by Teresa Southwick

An Unexpected Partnership
What Makes a Father

The Bachelors of Blackwater Lake

Finding Family...and Forever?
One Night with the Boss
The Rancher Who Took Her In
A Decent Proposal
The Widow's Bachelor Bargain
How to Land Her Lawman
A Word with the Bachelor
Just a Little Bit Married
The New Guy in Town

Montana Mavericks:
The Lonelyhearts Ranch

Unmasking the Maverick

Montana Mavericks:
What Happened at the Wedding?

An Officer and a Maverick

Maverick
Holiday Magic

TERESA
SOUTHWICK

MILLS & BOON

First published in Great Britain 2019
by Mills & Boon, an imprint of HarperCollins*Publishers*
1 London Bridge Street, London, SE1 9GF

Large Print edition 2019

© 2019 Harlequin Books S.A.

Special thanks and acknowledgement are given to
Teresa Southwick for her contribution to the
Montana Mavericks: Six Brides for Six Brothers series.

ISBN: 978-0-263-08354-5

MIX
Paper from
responsible sources
FSC® C007454

Printed and bound in Great Britain
by CPI Group (UK) Ltd, Croydon, CR0 4YY

To all the remarkably creative
and talented writers
in the Montana Mavericks series
and our gifted and patient editor,
Susan Litman. All of you
made working on this book a joy!

Chapter One

Ambling A Ranch
Rust Creek Falls, Montana

Hunter Crawford knew what his father was up to.

It was common knowledge that Max had hired the local wedding planner to find wives for his six sons. Four of them were now off the marriage market and the target on Hunter's back was getting bigger. That's why he was suspicious of the old man pushing this big destination wedding for their brother Finn in Rustler's Notch, Colorado.

Hunter was pushing back. He'd much rather stay here on the Ambling A Ranch, where he was more insulated from his father's meddling.

There were four cabins on this sprawling property—the big house, where his father and his brother Wilder lived, and three smaller places.

Hunter lived in one of them with his six-year-old daughter, Wren, and loved the two-story log house. It had four bedrooms, two baths, a great room and kitchen. The place wasn't huge, but it had enough room for the two of them. The biggest selling point was that it had no bad memories from the past clinging to it. He was doing his best to keep the vibe pure of pain, for Wren's sake. Although that could change.

His instinct was telling him that this wedding was somehow going to threaten his resolve to maintain his bachelor designation. The way he saw it, everyone had one great love in their life and he'd had his. Losing her had nearly destroyed him. He was determined not to put himself in a position where that could happen to him again. But his father and Wilder weren't taking no for an answer and had come to give him a hard sell.

He'd reluctantly opened the door to them and they followed him into the kitchen. Might as well get this over with, he told himself as he took a breath and faced them. "I'm not going to the wedding."

Maximilian Crawford stood beside the circular oak table and stared him down. He was a tall, handsome, distinguished man in his sixties. Tan and rugged looking, his lined face suggested a life spent outdoors—and it had been. Now he left the physically taxing ranch work to Hunter and his brothers. His hair had once been brown like his sons' but now it was gray and earned him the nickname "Silver Fox." He was accustomed to getting what he wanted by any legal means necessary, but Hunter had inherited his father's stubborn streak. So neither of them blinked.

Finally, his father said, "Why?"

"I have my reasons."

"It's important to me that the whole family is there. Your brothers and their new wives are looking forward to a little vacation in Rustler's Notch." The older man looked at his youngest son, a "don't just stand there" expression in his eyes.

"Yeah," Wilder said. "You could use a vacation, bro."

"I'm good," Hunter said.

"It's actually not you I'm worried about." Wilder settled his hands on his lean hips. "The truth is, I could use your help. The two of us are the only single Crawford men left. It's Colorado in November. Can you say 'snow bunnies'? It pains me to say this, but I need a wingman."

Hunter glared at him. "Did someone drop you on your head when you were a baby?"

"Maybe." Wilder glanced at their father, then shrugged. "Why?"

"Just to make sure I've got this right…" He paused for dramatic effect. "At this family outing, your primary goal is to hit on every single woman between the ages of twenty and forty?"

"Yes."

It wasn't easy to get under his brother's skin. Hunter wasn't even sure why he tried. "Even if I was interested in partying, which I'm not, I have a six-year-old daughter. Wren and I would cramp your style."

"I wasn't suggesting we bring Wren." Wilder stopped for a moment, clearly thinking that over. "Although, a single father with a kid could be a chick magnet."

"Don't even go there," Hunter warned. "And no, you can't borrow her."

"That's low," his brother said. "I would never use my niece like that."

"He was just kidding," Max cut in.

"Yeah, lighten up, big brother. It would do you good to let off some steam."

"How would you know?" Hunter asked. "All you think about is your next score. You have absolutely no responsibilities. And no idea what I've gone through."

"That's true," Wilder acknowledged. "But

it's been six years since your wife died. Everyone else has been tiptoeing around the subject but I'm already in the doghouse with you so what the heck."

"What are you talking about?"

"Lara wouldn't want you to be like this. There's no law against moving on. And your daughter should see you out and having fun."

"He's right, son." Max's expression was sympathetic.

Hunter shifted his glare to Max. "You don't get a vote."

Max's wife, the brothers' mother, had left the family without a word when Hunter was a little boy and Wilder was just a baby. Their father was on his own raising six boys. As a kid, Hunter didn't know that his parents' relationship was bitterly unhappy. All he knew was that his mother took off and he'd believed if he'd been a better kid, a better son, she would have stayed. Max had it rough but Sheila didn't die. She'd made a choice. Unlike Hunter's wife, who'd passed away suddenly. The woman he'd loved was gone forever and there was no one to blame but himself.

"It's true," Max said. "I can't tell you what to do. But that doesn't change the fact that I would really like to celebrate your brother's marriage with my whole family in attendance."

"Why is this wedding such a big deal to you, Dad?"

Max sighed and looked the way he always did when something should be clear as day but he still had to explain. "Sarah and Logan had a nontraditional ceremony at the local bar."

"Nothing wrong with Ace in the Hole. I've met some nice women there," Wilder said.

Max shook his head and continued. "Xander and Lily had their wedding at the Rust Creek Falls Community Center."

"It was nice. My daughter had a great time there." It was local and this town was a place where everyone watched out for neighbors. Hunter didn't have to worry about keeping an eye on Wren every second.

"Knox and Genevieve were secretly married," Max continued.

"So were Finn and Avery," Hunter interjected. "I say again—what's the big deal?"

"I think it's about time we had a big splashy, formal family affair. We have a lot to celebrate, what with four of you boys settled down." Max was known to be a master manipulator, but no one doubted his love for his sons. "Think about it. Five-star resort. Beautiful country. Love in the air."

Maybe for his brothers, but Hunter wasn't interested in love. Not again. "Look, Dad, how many ways do you want me to say this? I don't want to meet anyone. Stop trying to fix me up and call off Vivienne Dalton."

"Matchmaking is not what this is about." Max didn't look the least bit guilty about paying the local wedding planner a million dollars to find wives for his six sons. "And think of your daughter. Think about Wren."

"She's all I think about." She was his world and everything he did was to keep her happy and safe.

"Why would you deny her the opportunity to be with her family? To make memories. And if you were to have a little fun, too, well…" Max let the words hang in the air between them.

"And Finn asked you to be a groomsman along with the rest of us brothers," Wilder reminded him. "Come on, Hunter. You can't let him down. And as far as watching Wren? You've got Logan, Knox, Xander."

"And me," Max said.

"And me," Wilder chimed in.

"Yeah," Hunter said, deliberately surrounding the single word with sarcasm. "Because nothing could go wrong with that scenario."

"That's low," Wilder said. "If you can't trust your family, then who can you trust?"

"A nanny."

Hunter looked at his brother, then both of them stared at Max, who had made the suggestion. "What?"

"Hire a nanny for the wedding." Max shrugged.

"Wedding? What wedding?" No one had

seen Wren standing there. But now the little girl was clearly excited. "Can I be in it? The bride and groom are going to need a flower girl."

"Oh, sugar. I'm in deep trouble now," Hunter muttered to himself.

"Hi, Gramps." The blonde, blue-eyed star of his world walked farther into the room and looked way up at the tall men surrounding her. "Hi, Uncle Wilder. I was upstairs playing with my princess dolls. I didn't know you were here."

Max went down on one knee to be on her level. "Hi, Wrennie. We came to talk to your dad about going to Uncle Finn's wedding. I'm going to use my private plane to fly us all there and we're going to stay in a very fancy hotel."

"Oh, boy!" Her big eyes grew bigger. "For real?"

"Yup. And I'm pretty sure Avery is going to ask you to be her flower girl. But your dad isn't sure he wants to go."

She turned her gaze on him. "But why?"

Hunter hated when she looked at him like this. He lost every argument because stubborn was no match for those big blue eyes. "It's a town that's bigger than Rust Creek Falls. In a hotel like that there are lots of tourists—"

"Who?"

"Strangers visiting from everywhere. It will be harder for me to keep an eye on you all the time."

"But the flower girl gets to wear a pretty dress. Not as pretty as Avery's because she's the bride and that's like the wedding princess, but…"

"I suppose." Hunter was at a loss when she talked dresses.

"And maybe Avery doesn't know anyone else to be a flower girl," Wren said earnestly. "I have to be there."

"That's a good point." Wilder bent at the waist and rested his hands on his knees, making his gaze almost level with hers. "And there's something else you should know. Your dad is supposed to be Uncle Finn's groomsman."

"Would you have to get all dressed up, too?" the little girl asked.

"That's right, Wren," Max said. "Your daddy is going to need a tuxedo."

This was why his dad and Wilder had followed him here to the house to finish this discussion. Despite their words to the contrary, they knew Wren was home from school. The two of them were counting on her to overhear. With her on their side, he didn't stand a chance. But he'd give it one more shot.

"If I'm in the wedding, honey, it means I can't watch over you the way I want."

Wren nodded thoughtfully, then her face brightened. "I heard Gramps say something about getting someone to take care of me."

"Yeah, but I don't think we can find anyone on such short notice." Hunter was beginning to hope there was a way for him to make this situation work in his favor after all.

"I know someone," his daughter said.

Well, dang it. "Who?"

"Miss Merry. She works at my school. She helps in the classroom and she's a playground supervisor at recess and lunch." She smiled. "She's really nice, especially on my first day of school when I was new. She played with me and got the other kids to play, too. She's my first best friend in Rust Creek Falls."

"She sounds perfect," Max approved. "You're not going to disappoint my granddaughter, are you, Hunter?"

"Please, Daddy."

The eyes, the pleading voice. The guilt that she didn't have a mother. Hunter was toast and he knew it. "I'll talk to Miss Merry and see what she says. But if it doesn't work out, that's it. Will you be okay with that?"

"Yes!" Wren threw herself into his arms. "Thank you, Daddy. You're the best daddy in the whole world."

If only. He wanted to be her hero and keep her safe. So he would meet Miss Merry, who sounded like someone's elderly grandmother. In which case this could work.

* * *

"You're younger than I thought you'd be."

And you're even more handsome than you sounded on the phone. For a split second Merry Matthews was afraid she'd said that out loud. When the wariness in his green eyes didn't change to fear of the crazy woman, she figured the thought stayed in her head where it belonged.

She'd heard rumors in town about his exceptional good looks, but she had been woefully unprepared to see Hunter Crawford in the flesh. Then his deep voice had her nerve endings sparking and momentarily shorted out a commonsense answer. Now he was staring at her as if her hair was on fire. It was time to say something.

"I'm Meredith Matthews but everyone calls me Merry." She was standing on the front porch of his log cabin house on the Ambling A Ranch. The man practically filled the doorway and she was looking up at him. "And I'm not sure how to respond to that remark about my age, Mr. Crawford."

"Sorry. It's just that my daughter talked about you and I just expected—" He shook his head and looked sheepish and, actually, pretty adorable. A dashing cowboy dressed in a snap-front shirt, worn jeans and boots. There was probably a Stetson around somewhere but he wasn't wearing it. His short hair was light brown and there was the slightest indentation in his chin. "I apologize. That was rude."

"Not really. If you think about it, there's no way to go wrong when you judge a woman's age on the younger side."

"I suppose that's true enough. But now I've kept you standing outside in the cold. Please come in." He opened the heavy door wider and stepped back to let her enter.

Merry glanced at the interior and liked what she saw. There were wood floors with colorful braided rugs strategically scattered over the surface. A comfortable blue couch and a leather recliner were arranged in front of a flat screen TV housed in an entertainment center. On the opposite wall a fireplace held freshly chopped wood just waiting for a match to light it. The place had a woodsy feel and was very cozy.

When she looked at the man again, any hint of sheepishness had disappeared, and he was all business. Which he should be. After all, this was a job interview.

"Please have a seat." He indicated the sofa and took the chair at a right angle to it. "As I said on the phone, Wren mentioned you for a child-care position that I need to fill."

"I'm looking forward to hearing more about it." She really needed the money and appreciated this chance.

What she made as an aide at Rust Creek Falls Elementary School didn't go far enough now. Since her father's death, she'd had to shut down his electrician business and there went her extra income. This could be the break she so badly needed.

She settled her purse beside her and rested the folder she'd brought on her knees. "How can I help you?"

"My brother is getting married in a couple

of weeks. It's a destination wedding, in Colorado. A place called Rustler's Notch. Have you heard of it?"

She shook her head. "Sounds quaint and colorful. And interesting."

Exasperation flashed in his eyes, a clue that there was a story here. "Mostly it's inconvenient."

"How so?"

"My father is sparing no expense and insists the whole family be there."

"That's very generous of him. And I can see how you'd think it's incredibly unreasonable," she teased. "Is there a problem?"

Irritation flashed in his eyes again but this time it was directed at her. "I have five brothers. Four of them are married. One has a baby. They've offered to help keep an eye on Wren and have the best of intentions, but all of them have distractions. The bottom line is that she's my responsibility. My daughter is at that stage where she's curious and likes to explore, and while I like to think

I can keep up with her, sometimes one person isn't enough."

Merry had taken his daughter under her wing on her first day of school. Wren had been new to town and frightened and Merry understood how that felt because growing up she'd been the new kid a lot. Her father had moved around for work and she'd changed schools often. So it had become her mission to make Wren Crawford comfortable, introduce her to the other kids and facilitate friendships. The little girl had made passing comments about her life. Her mother was dead and her father was sad sometimes.

She folded her hands and set them on the file folder in her lap. "Wild guess here. You don't want to go to the wedding."

He grinned wryly. "And I thought I was being subtle. To be honest, I'd rather not. But I can't let my daughter miss out on the chance to be a flower girl, which she wants more than another princess doll. Also I'm a groomsman, so..."

"You don't feel you have much choice."

"Yes. And—" His gaze narrowed.

Merry had the fleeting thought that his intensity brought out a dark, brooding and slightly dangerous side that made her insides quiver. And that reaction needed to stay inside if she was going to land this gig. "Is something wrong?"

"You're judging," he accused.

"I'm not," she lied. "Just clarifying. Trying to determine your expectations for the child-care professional you're looking to hire."

He nodded. "Because of the commitments I have at the event, it will be impossible for me to keep an eye on Wren one hundred percent of the time, and while of course I want someone to watch her when I can't, it would be great if that person could really relate to her." His mouth pulled tight for a moment. "I want someone who is nurturing, caring and warm with my daughter." Another slight grin ghosted across his face. "No self-defense training is required."

"Your little girl is an angel. I think I can

handle the above qualifications without breaking a sweat."

"Wren really seems to like you. But she's a kid. How do I know you're the best person for this position?"

"I brought references." Based on the few things his daughter had said, she'd had a feeling she might need more than just her sincere and friendly smile to get this job. She handed him the folder.

He opened it and glanced through the papers there. "What's this?"

"My résumé. Also I've included business, personal and educational references." They were all glowing declarations of her interaction with people in general and children in particular.

One by one he examined each testimonial. "You're an aide at the school, taking early childhood education classes. And you work for your father's electrical business."

"Not anymore. He passed away recently."

His gaze met hers and there was sincere

sympathy in his eyes. "I'm sorry for your loss."

"Thank you." The words were quiet and polite, completely at odds with the pain and panic of insecurity trickling through her.

He nodded, then continued his inspection of her paperwork. "This all looks to be in order. Do you have anything else?"

Really? Apparently he was looking to hire Mother Teresa. She reached for her purse and pulled out her wallet. "Did you miss the part in the principal's letter of recommendation where she mentioned my wings, halo and uncanny ability to walk on water? Here's my current Montana driver's license. Feel free to run a background check."

Merry had kept her tone courteous and professional, though she wanted to be huffy and annoyed. Still, she prepared herself to be shown out of his house. Her recommendations were glowing. That wasn't blowing her own horn, just a fact. If that wasn't good enough for him, then maybe the extra money wasn't worth the trouble. And good luck to him finding a weekend nanny in this town.

The man stared at her for several moments before the corners of his mouth curved up a little. He was fighting a smile. Hallelujah. The cowboy had a sense of humor.

"That won't be necessary, Miss Matthews. The most important qualification for this job isn't on here."

"And that is?"

"Wren likes you. If you still want it, the position is yours."

She looked at him for a moment, not sure she'd heard right. "You're sure? As you probably guessed from what I said, I can sometimes be headstrong and a little outspoken."

"I noticed. And you may have guessed that I am protective of my daughter. Maybe too much, but with her I'd rather be safe than sorry."

"You love her," Merry said simply. And it was quite possibly his most attractive quality.

"I do. Very much. Her mother died so she only has me."

"She told me." Merry remembered the conversation. She'd told Wren her own mom was gone, too, and that made them members of a club that no little girl wanted to join.

"Okay. That means you understand the situation." He handed back her folder. "So, will you take the job?"

"Yes. I'd love to," she said. "And I really wanted it. A chance to earn some extra money *and* the chance to get away for a couple of days at the same time. It's been a rough year for me. So, yes. Thank you for the opportunity, Mr. Crawford."

"If you call me that, I'll be looking around for my father. It's Hunter."

"Okay."

"May I call you Merry?" he asked.

"Wren already does so that works for me."

"All right, then. I'll give you the details."

Hunter explained that his father's private jet would take them to Rustler's Notch, where they'd stay in a three-bedroom suite at the hotel. He told her the salary and the amount was exceptionally generous. Now it was her turn to fight a smile. She would be expected to keep Wren in sight at all times, which meant attending the rehearsal dinner and wedding festivities the next day.

"Oh, this is probably relevant information for you since my daughter is over the moon about the fancy flower girl dress she will wear. The ceremony is formal."

The scenario he described was like a fantasy, until he dropped that bombshell. She didn't have anything to wear to a formal wedding and there was no money in her extremely limited budget for a new dress.

"Is something wrong?" He was frowning at her.

"No. Why do you ask?"

"I don't know. Just a funny expression on your face. Are you okay?"

"Fine." She gave him a bright smile. And without missing a beat said, "That won't be a problem at all."

Nowhere in her personal references had

anyone said she was a habitual liar but that was the second whopper she'd told him. The first being that she wasn't judging him. How she wished this was a fairy tale. Then she could count on her fairy godmother spinning her a gorgeous dress out of unicorn sighs.

How in the world was she going to pull this off?

Chapter Two

Merry left the Ambling A just as the sun was dropping behind the mountains. She was in a panic and did what she always did at a time like this. She called her best friend, Zoey Kubiak, who was the other educational aide at the school. Zoey was a semester away from a degree in elementary education and lived with her divorced mother in a little house that had been restored after the Great Flood of 2013. In fact, they'd met when her dad did electrical work for Zoey's mom, Dora. She and her friend had sort of hoped their parents might click romantically, but that had never happened.

She pulled her dad's beat-up old truck to a stop at the curb in front of the gray house. Envy, worry and pain twisted inside her and she missed her father so much. If only he was here so she could talk to him. But, as he'd always said, if wishes were horses beggars would ride.

Merry slid out of the truck and walked up the sidewalk to the front door. It was opened before she could even knock.

"I hate it when you declare an emergency over the phone then say I'll tell you all about it when I get there." Zoey had long straight blond hair and cornflower blue eyes. She was beautiful, loyal, supportive—like the sister Merry had always wanted.

She hugged her friend. "I have a big problem."

"So you said. Together we will find a big solution. My mom is out for the evening so we have the house to ourselves. I put a casserole in the oven and a bottle of white wine is chilling. You'll spend the night and whatever is wrong can be fixed. I promise."

"I didn't bring my pajamas," Merry said.

Zoey shook her head. "Out of everything I said that was your takeaway?"

"I'm overwhelmed."

"You came to the right place. We're about the same size so you can wear a pair of my jammies."

"You don't happen to have a cocktail dress lying around, do you?" It was a joke, a throwaway remark, a sign of desperation.

"As a matter of fact, I do have a couple." Zoey studied her face. "What's wrong, Mer?"

"I think we're going to need that wine for this."

"Okay. Follow me."

They went into the small but cute kitchen with white cabinets and wood floors. Zoey opened the bottle, then poured the golden liquid into two stemless glasses before they sat down at the dinette.

"Now, tell me everything."

Merry sucked in a breath, then let it out. "I just left a job interview with Hunter Crawford. He needs a nanny for the weekend. His brother is getting married at a fancy resort in Colorado—"

"Rustler's Notch?"

"Yes." Merry stared. "How did you know?"

"It's the new 'in' place for weddings. I read an article about it in a bridal magazine. Looks like a gorgeous spot. Romantic." The excitement level in Zoey's voice rose as she talked. "And Hunter Crawford is going to pay you to go there with him?"

"His whole family is going and he's paying me to take care of his daughter for the weekend."

"Isn't she the little cutie who gives you a hug every morning at school?"

"Yes. She's a sweetheart, so smart and loving." Merry smiled. "Watching her will be a pleasure. Besides, I really need the extra money. It's an all-expenses-paid trip combined with a paycheck, which makes it kind of a dream job."

Zoey looked puzzled. "I'm still not seeing the problem."

"It's a formal wedding, Zo. I don't have anything to wear to something like that. And I don't have the money to buy anything. So it's a catch-22. What am I going to do? I have to go to the ceremony. Hunter really needs me there to keep an eye on Wren because he'll be busy with groomsman stuff and family."

Zoey tapped her lip. "Well, as I said, you've come to the right place. I've been in friends' weddings—always a bridesmaid, never a bride, as the saying goes. You and I are pretty close to the same size. Come on. Let's go play dress up."

Merry basically had nothing to lose. She followed her friend down the hall to the bedroom. It was a very girlie space with pink bedspread, flowered throw pillows and lace curtains crisscrossed over the window. From the walk-in closet Zoey pulled out four heavy-duty hangers holding long dresses.

While Merry stripped out of her slacks and

sweater the other woman removed the plastic protecting the first dress, a black number with long sleeves. It fit, but neither of them was crazy about it. The next was yellow, but an unflattering shade that washed out her skin. Number three was orange.

Zoey took one look and grimaced. "It was a Halloween wedding. I don't even know why I keep it. Take that off and we will never speak of it again."

"Thank God." Merry did as ordered while her friend took the plastic off dress number four—also known as her last hope. "Well, the black one will work although neither of us thought it was a wow. Still it's... Wow." She got a look at the pale lavender dress Zoey was holding up. "That color is fabulous."

"It will bring out your hazel eyes. And, I confess, this one is my favorite. I've been saving it for last. And I have shoes to match. I'll find them." She disappeared back into the closet.

Merry slid the chiffon over her head and

loved the silky feel of the fabric flowing over her body. It was a one-shoulder dress with a floaty skirt, a satin sash and it fit like a dream.

Zoey reappeared with a shoe box in hand and stopped dead in her tracks to stare. "Oh, Mer, that looks fantastic."

"Really?" She thought so but desperation could skew a girl's fashion sense. But in her opinion it was definitely fairy-godmother worthy.

"It looks better on you than me and it looked pretty awesome on me."

Merry moved around the room, then back to the freestanding full-length mirror. "Do you think the slit is too revealing? After all, Hunter hired me as the nanny. I'm not sure if there's a dress code."

"It hits you mid-thigh," Zoey said, studying her critically. "It's not immodest and your legs are great. I think it's fine. Is another brother getting married? The last I heard Finn and Avery had eloped."

"They did. But their father wants a big

family celebration for them since the other three weddings were casual."

"He's number four out of six to find true love here in Rust Creek Falls. It would seem that the Crawford bachelors are dropping like flies since coming to town. So, tell me about Hunter." There was a gleam in her friend's eyes.

Merry should have expected this and had an answer ready, but she'd been preoccupied with her wardrobe crisis. Her reaction to him had been instant and visceral—sweaty palms, weak knees, pounding heart. For some reason she was reluctant to share that. Maybe because he'd been very businesslike and serious, but when he smiled… That was a moment with a capital *M.* "What do you want to know?"

"Everything. He's elusive. According to the rumor mill he's never in town by himself, always with his daughter."

"Well, I like him," Merry said. "And don't start. It's not in a crush sort of way. He's a concerned father or I wouldn't have this job."

"I talked to Vivienne Dalton who knows all of the Crawfords. Hunter is a widower and she said he's just as good-looking as the other brothers. Did you get a sense that he's looking to settle down like the others?" Zoey asked.

"No." Merry got exactly the opposite feeling. The man didn't even want to go to the wedding. And her instincts told her that wasn't just about logistics with child care for Wren. "I think his daughter is the only female he's interested in."

"Too bad. Shame for all that hunk factor to go to waste." Zoey sighed. "But I guess dating is hard when you have a child."

"Dating is hard when you don't." Even Merry heard the bitterness in her voice.

"Oh, shoot. I didn't mean to remind you of him." Zoey handed her the shoes to try on.

"You mean Ken? The guy who dumped me when my dad was going through cancer treatment? The one who couldn't say good-bye fast enough because he didn't come first?"

"Yeah. Him."

"You know my dad had very strong opinions on every guy I dated. Not like he hated them all, but he knew the good ones from the bad. And he didn't like Ken Michaelson from the moment they met."

"And he was right on the money. That jerk deserted you when you needed him most," Zoey commented.

"Yet another example that men aren't especially loyal. Even my brother, Jack."

"He's in the military," Zoey reminded her.

"I know. The thing is he joined right after my mom died when I was just a little girl. Dad and I hardly ever saw him and he barely made it home for my father's funeral. So he's pretty much disappeared and that doesn't meet my definition of loyal." She stepped into the pale lavender shoes. "They're a little big."

"Stuff tissues in the toes. They'll be fine," Zoey said. "And I've got a strapless bra, so don't worry about that. I think you're good to go."

"You are a life saver. Dependable and true blue." Merry hugged her. "Unlike most men. Although Hunter's devotion to his daughter is refreshing. I like that."

"Oh, really?"

"Please. Don't start. For crying out loud it's just a weekend."

And now that she had a wedding outfit, it was a weekend she was looking forward to.

Hunter slowed the SUV until he found the address Merry had given him and came to a stop in front of her small yellow house with white trim. There was an old truck in the driveway with Matthews Electrical written on the side of it. He'd promised to pick her up for the flight to Colorado that would take them to his brother's wedding.

"Well," he said to Wren, "this is the place."

"Daddy, I'm going to get Miss Merry." Wren was out of the car before he could stop her.

Hunter turned off the engine, jumped out of the vehicle and followed his daughter up the sidewalk to the porch. He noticed a for sale sign on a sturdy white post prominently displayed in the neatly trimmed front grass. That bothered him a little and it shouldn't because he barely knew the woman. But Wren liked her and he wasn't in favor of any changes that could potentially affect her happiness.

The door opened before he could knock and Merry was there, a smile on her face as bright as the cheery yellow paint on her house. Hunter felt a thump in his chest, one hard whack that seemed to jump-start his heart.

"Good morning, Wren. Hunter."

"Hi, Miss Merry. We're goin' on Gramps's jet. He's taking the whole family on it. Have you ever been on a jet?"

"Yes. Once. But it was a commercial flight, not private. This is very exciting."

"I can't wait." His daughter was practically quivering with anticipation.

"We're running late," Hunter said. "But if you need a little more time, I guarantee they'll hold the plane for the flower girl. Maximilian Crawford will make sure of that."

Merry smiled up at him. "I'm ready to go. My suitcase is right here by the door. My dress is in a garment bag. Is that okay?"

Before he could say it was fine, Wren jumped in.

"Daddy and me have that, too. My dress is so pretty. I'm gonna look like a princess. Right, Daddy?"

"Honey, you look like a princess to me no matter what you wear."

Love expanded inside him when she smiled up at him like that, as if he was her hero. Then he looked at Merry and felt that whack in his chest again. Her blond hair was a mass of curls, and enthusiasm sparkled in her hazel eyes. There was a flush of pink on her cheeks that could be about the chill in the air or the beginning of an adventure. Whatever the cause, he was oddly reluctant to stop looking at her.

"Should we get going?" Merry asked.

That snapped him out of it. They were late. "I'll get your suitcase."

"Thanks." She backed up and let him reach inside to grab the handle of the bag that had seen better days. "I'll get my dress."

"What can I carry?" Wren asked.

Merry thought for a moment. "Why don't you hold my purse while I lock the door?"

"Okay." The little girl took the big bag. "This is heavy."

"It is. Set it on the porch, sweetie." She locked up, then took her purse for the walk to the car.

Hunter hit a button on his key fob and the SUV hatch slowly lifted. He put her bag in the back with the other two, then took her dress and settled it on the rear passenger hook. "Okay, ladies. Let's roll."

"I have to sit in the back in my car seat, Miss Merry. Daddy says so."

"It's safer for you, sweetie."

"That's what he says, too."

"Do you want me to sit back there with you?"

Wren thought for a moment then said, "No. It's nice for him to have someone to talk to until I'm big enough to sit in the front with him."

That settled that. They all got in and buckled up. It wasn't often there was a woman—a beautiful woman—riding in his front passenger seat. This was different—not bad different, just enough for him to feel a little tongue-tied. Fortunately his daughter picked up the conversation slack.

"We're goin' to Billings. That's where the airport is. I brought my princess bride doll with me."

"That seems very appropriate for this occasion," Merry said.

"My dress is prettier than hers. But she has a tiara. I asked Aunt Avery if I could wear one and she said she didn't think it would go with my dress."

"It was a diplomatic no," Hunter said so only Merry could hear. She laughed, then covered it with a cough.

"I wish I could wear one." Wren sighed

and it was loud enough to be heard over the road noise. "Daddy says I'm his princess and everyone knows princesses wear tiaras."

"That makes sense," Merry said thoughtfully. "But a princess is always sensitive to the feelings of people around her. And this is going to be your aunt Avery's special day when she marries your uncle Finn. A princess would never do anything to spoil a bride's wedding day. Don't you think so, Wren?"

That got a grudging "I guess so" and Hunter was impressed by the way Merry handled that situation. When they arrived at the airport he parked at the terminal where they would board his father's Gulfstream jet. The crew met them and took their luggage before Hunter, Merry and Wren walked up the steps and into the aircraft.

Hunter waved to everyone on board and a quick head count indicated they were the last ones to arrive. He started to make introductions but was interrupted by an announcement to take their seats and fasten seat belts in preparation for takeoff. The plush leather and teak-trimmed cabin was configured with individual seats of four with a table in between to form a conversation area. There were also a couple of couches that would accommodate three and only one was left. His daughter plopped herself down on one end. That meant he and Merry would be sitting side by side. Unlike the front seat of his SUV, there would be no console between them.

"Sit next to me, Miss Merry."

"Okay."

Hunter took the empty space beside her and their shoulders brushed, their legs touched. He was grateful the stretchy pants she wore tucked into shin-high black boots meant her skin was not bare. When he fastened his seat belt, his fingers brushed her thigh, or more accurately the cream-colored sweater that covered her hips and butt. She smelled disarmingly female and sweet, a thought that sent a tsunami of testosterone crashing over him.

When everyone was secured, they received permission from the control tower to taxi down the runway and in seconds they were off. As soon as the seat belt sign was turned off, Wren bounced up and said she was going to talk to Aunt Avery and tell her she didn't mind not wearing a tiara.

More than almost anything Hunter wanted to move away from Merry but he didn't feel right about leaving her alone. They all knew he'd hired a nanny for the weekend but the noisy jet made introductions awkward. So, for the duration of the flight, he felt obligated to stay put and introduce her when they were on the ground.

Merry was looking around the interior, eyes wide. "I wonder where they keep the barf bags."

"You don't feel well?"

"I'm fine actually." She laughed but there was a little uncertainty on her face. "It's just nerves. When I get this way, I say weird things. Helps break the tension."

"Okay."

"In fact they probably don't even have barf bags. Most likely there's a rule against getting sick on the expensive leather seats."

"Let them try to enforce that one," Hunter said.

"I know, right?" She glanced a little anxiously at the rest of his family, chatting together in groups. "There are a lot of Crawfords on this plane."

"Yeah. I'm sorry about not introducing you to all of them. I'll take care of that when we land."

"No problem. I'm just the hired help, after all." She was still looking around the luxurious interior with an expression of awe that made her eyes look more green than brown.

"If we weren't in such a rush, I'd have made sure they all met you. It's my fault we were running late."

She looked skeptical. "Something tells me your daughter was responsible for that. I know her from school, remember?"

"Yeah." It was one of the reasons he'd hired her.

"I feel like I need to pinch myself. Maybe I should be paying *you*. I can't believe I'm flying in a private jet. If anyone had told me I'd be doing this, I'd have said they were crazy. People with money really do live differently."

"I suppose."

His gaze drifted to his daughter, the child he'd raised alone almost from the day she was born. Money didn't guarantee you wouldn't lose the mother of your baby girl. He would give up everything he had in a heartbeat if it could bring Lara back.

"I'm sorry."

"Hmm?" He looked at Merry.

"That was unprofessional of me. It was tactless to say that."

He thought her comments were honest and charming. "Why would you think so?"

"It seems as if I've heard you should never discuss money and politics." She tucked her hair behind her ear. "Again, I plead nerves. Apparently getting up at the crack of dawn has disengaged the filter between my brain and my mouth. That's my story and I'm sticking to it."

He smiled, but the movement felt rusty when directed at a woman. It seemed wrong somehow, but he couldn't seem to stop. "Your unfiltered frankness is refreshing."

It seemed her condition was contagious because things were popping out of his mouth, too. Was that crossing a line between employer and employee? If Merry was a ranch hand, he would know where the line was. And it wasn't as if he hadn't had child care before. When Wren was a baby, he'd hired help from time to time. He had to work the ranch, after all. But with Merry he felt strongly about keeping boundaries firmly in place.

"Calling what I said frankness is generous of you," she said. "I always thought of the word *decadent* in terms of dessert. But this experience has broadened the definition for me. However, I will, at some point, get over how special it feels to fly in a private jet."

"You can thank my dad."

"I will, of course."

He laughed. "I didn't mean that literally. Just that it was important to him that this be a fun family event from start to finish."

"You can count on me. I'll take good care of Wren so you can enjoy yourself this weekend."

He already was. With her. And that realization surprised and bothered him. It was almost a relief when the captain announced they were starting their descent into the airport in Rustler's Notch, Colorado. The flight time had, no pun intended, flown. Talking to Merry was pleasant. And distracting. More than he'd expected. Definitely more than he wanted.

It was disconcerting and uncomfortable when he realized he was caught between not wanting the flight to end and being grateful that it had been so short. That was the classic definition of conflict. He didn't like conflict, especially when a woman was involved.

Chapter Three

Merry was a little nervous when the plane landed, then taxied closer to the terminal. Her responsibilities were going to kick in and part of that would be interacting with the Crawfords. Time to put on her big girl panties and a friendly smile. The seat belt sign dinged off and everyone in the cabin stood to gather their belongings. They filed down the stairs and stood in a group not far from the plane.

"Listen up, everyone," Hunter said. "Before we all split up, I want to introduce you to Meredith Matthews—"

"She's Miss Merry," Wren interjected.

Merry lifted her hand to wave everyone a friendly greeting, at the same time hating all the focus on her. "Hi."

Hunter introduced his brothers and their wives one by one. She had already guessed who Avery and Finn were because Wren had spent a good portion of the flight talking princess with the bride. Max, the tall, handsome, silver-haired patriarch, was impossible to forget. But everyone else sort of blurred together.

"There are a lot of you," she said ruefully. "I think you need to wear name tags."

Everyone laughed and assured her there would be no hard feelings for a name mix-up. Then Hunter's father directed the group to the three limousines waiting to take them to Rustler's Notch Resort.

"Don't we need to get our luggage?" Merry asked when they all started to move.

"It will be delivered to our rooms," Hunter assured her. The doubt must have shown on her face because he added, "I promise it will be fine. And yes, rich people do live differently."

"You took the words right out of my mouth. But if I don't have my pajamas—"

"I will buy you whatever you need if I'm wrong."

"Fair enough."

Following Max's instructions, the process was smooth and efficient. He and his youngest son, Wilder, climbed into the car with Hunter, Wren and Merry.

"Mr. Crawford," she said to the family patriarch, "I would like to thank you for this weekend. I will take excellent care of your granddaughter."

The man winked at the little girl, who'd insisted on sitting beside him. "Wrennie is very special to me."

"I can see that, sir."

"It will go to his head if you call him that," Wilder teased her. He looked like a charming rogue, handsome with longish brown hair and piercing dark eyes.

Merry could picture him breaking hearts

everywhere he went. He was one of those men most women would be attracted to. Although she wasn't. Glancing sideways at Hunter, she felt a little flutter in her chest that indicated she couldn't say the same about his older brother.

The scenery on the short drive to the hotel was breathtaking. Trees, rugged mountains and blue sky added up to a spectacularly beautiful day. They passed ski slopes but it was early November and there wasn't enough snow yet for them to open. Before long the resort buildings came into view and the car stopped in front. The hotel tower was tall, all wood and beams with a peaked roof that looked chalet-like and just right for this environment.

Merry had never been anywhere like this. Not ever. She was speechless, but Wren did enough chattering for both of them. Following behind the Crawford clan she was able to observe Hunter with his daughter. The trusting way the little girl slipped her small hand into his bigger one. He teased her before effortlessly lifting her onto his broad shoulders as they walked into the spectacular lobby with its wood floors and huge fireplace, where logs cheerfully burned and crackled.

Apparently having money also made check-in a breeze because room keys were waiting and bags had indeed been delivered to the suites. Max instructed everyone to go have fun and they would meet later in the afternoon for the wedding rehearsal followed by dinner. Hunter had already assured Merry she would have her own room, but she wasn't clear on how that would logistically work with a suite. After an elevator ride to the top floor, he unlocked the door and they walked in.

There was a beautifully decorated living room that separated the master and auxiliary bedrooms from the one on the opposite side of the suite. She would have her privacy and still be available to Wren if needed. And, as Hunter had promised, her suitcase was there on the bench at the end of the king bed. Her borrowed dress was hanging in the closet. Quite possibly this hotel suite was bigger than her entire house back in Rust Creek Falls.

Wren ran into Merry's room and grabbed her hand. "Come and see where I'm going to sleep."

Merry let herself be tugged into the room. The puffy mattress was high and the white bedding looked pristine. "This is beautiful. Fit for a princess."

"Come and see Daddy's room. It's way bigger."

That seemed too intimate, too much an invasion of his privacy. Too tempting to think about him and what he wore, or didn't wear, to bed. And her heart was beating just a little too fast, a sure sign doing this would be a bad idea.

"Why don't we unpack your suitcase? And I want to see your dress. It's probably hanging in the closet." Merry saw Hunter in the doorway and wondered what he was thinking with that brooding look on his face.

Wren folded her arms over her thin chest. "You can't see my dress until the wedding. Like the bride."

Merry laughed. "Fair enough. But we should still get your things unpacked. Make sure you have your shoes, tights and everything you need. There are good surprises and bad ones."

The child thought that over then nodded. "Okay."

They made short work of unpacking the small princess suitcase. Once the wedding day accessories were present and accounted for, the little girl started jumping on the bed.

"Wren, stop. You'll fall and hurt yourself," Hunter said sharply.

Merry knew this was pent-up energy and excitement, not bad behavior. It just needed to be channeled in a more positive way. She believed her job wasn't just about babysitting when Hunter wasn't around, but to help out whenever she could. This was one of those times.

"I have an idea," she said.

The child stopped jumping. "What?"

"We should go exploring."

"For what?" the little girl asked.

"Adventures. There are beautiful grounds here at the hotel. Just look out the window."

Wren plopped her bottom on the bed then slid off and raced over to the window. "I see a lake with water coming up out of the middle. And a sidewalk. And maybe a play area. Daddy, come and look. We should go."

"Sounds like a good start for an adventure. I'll take you," Merry said.

"No. I want Daddy to come, too."

"Maybe your dad wants to rest. After all, he was up pretty early this morning."

The little girl looked up at him. "Do you want to take a nap instead of exploring with me and Miss Merry?"

"Absolutely not." Although he didn't look quite that certain. "I wouldn't miss it."

"Yay!" Wren clapped her hands and headed for the door. "Let's go."

"Put on your jacket," Merry and Hunter said at the same time.

All of them grabbed coats and left the suite. After taking the elevator to the first floor they found the exit leading to the rear of the property and a path lined with shrubs. In her pink quilted jacket Wren took off running as her ponytail swung from side to side.

"Stay where I can see you," Hunter shouted.

"I will," she called back.

Merry walked beside her employer as they moved more slowly down the path. To fill a silence that bordered on awkward she asked, "How do you like Montana? And why did your family leave Texas?"

She glanced up at him and saw his mouth pull tight as a muscle in his cheek tensed. The question had stirred up something not good and she began to wonder if he was going to answer at all.

Finally he said, "When my dad gets an idea into his head it's pretty hard to change his mind."

"Did you want to?"

"I like ranch work, taking care of the animals. I don't much care what state I do it in.

As long as my daughter is happy, I'm good." He looked down. "Thanks to you, her school transition was smooth."

"I'm glad I could help. I know how it feels to be the new kid in the class." As they walked, Merry was keeping that pink jacket in sight and she figured Hunter was, too.

"You made the difference. Please tell me you're not leaving town."

"Why would you think I was?"

"I noticed the for sale sign in front of your house."

"Oh. No. I'm not leaving Rust Creek Falls," she said.

"Then why sell?"

Because she couldn't afford the monthly payments and that was humiliating to admit. Merry had faced a lot of speed bumps on the road to establishing her career, which meant that her bank account had suffered, too. She was torn about telling him the truth, then decided keeping it to herself might have him thinking it was something worse.

"My mother died when I was about Wren's

age. My brother is ten years older than me and he joined the military." She was the one dealing with memories now and they were sad. It had been a lonely time for her. There'd been no motherly hugs after school, no homemade cookies with a glass of cold milk. Her father had withdrawn into his own grief and she'd felt all alone. "Dad didn't quite know what to do with me so he took me to work with him a lot."

"What kind of work?"

"Electrician. Ed Matthews knew his way around wires and light switches. Not so much about what to do with a motherless little girl."

"I can relate to that."

"And we moved around a lot, going where the work was. Following the jobs. Changing schools all the time."

"That's why you knew how Wren felt, why you looked out for her when she was new to the school."

"Yes." She smiled up at him, then zeroed in on the pink jacket again. For some reason she wanted him to know she was working on her life even though that wasn't what he'd asked. "You're wondering what all this has to do with selling the house. I promise I'll get there."

"Okay."

"My education was choppy, which put me behind. Plus, I helped my dad with the business. Answering phones and making appointments. Keeping the books." It had helped bring them closer and she treasured that time more than ever now that he was gone. "I could only manage college classes part-time. And then in 2013, after the flood in Rust Creek Falls, Dad decided to move there. The damage was widespread and there was a real need for construction workers, plumbers and electricians. It's a friendly, close-knit community and we decided to stay. We bought a house and fixed it up."

"But?"

"How do you know there's a 'but'?" she asked.

"Because your house is for sale."

"Right. I mentioned when we met that my dad died recently. Cancer." She took a deep breath and met his gaze. "On top of missing him very much, without him there is no business or income. I don't make enough at my school job to keep up with the mortgage payments."

"I see." He was frowning. "What will you do when the house is sold?"

"Right now I'm more nervous about the selling process. I have a real estate agent but never handled a real estate transaction on my own, without my dad."

"The agent should explain everything but if you still have questions, my brother Logan has sold all kinds of property. He could probably help you out."

"Thanks. That's good to know."

"And you're still in school." Obviously he'd read and retained the information she'd given him during the employment interview.

"Not at the moment. I had to care for my dad and was barely able to finish the spring semester online. I didn't register for fall because he wasn't doing well. But I'm going back to it right after the holidays."

"And your major is early childhood education. Seems like a good fit." He stuck his hands into the pockets of his sheepskin jacket. "You're really tuned in to my daughter. She doesn't even seem to notice she's being handled."

"Diversion. Distraction. Let them think the idea is theirs. A hard no isn't easy to reverse."

"Tell me about it." The tone in his voice and the look on his face indicated he'd had some experience with that and it didn't go well.

And then she felt bad. "I'm sorry, Hunter. For dumping on you like that. For bending your ear and making it all about me. That was unprofessional."

"Well, I asked," he said gently. "And maybe you needed to talk about it. The grief, I mean."

Hmm. This "getting to know you" felt something like a first date. It wasn't, but that didn't stop her curiosity about him. When had Wren lost her mother? And how? The thing was, it didn't feel right to just come out and ask.

"Do you miss Texas?" she said instead.

"No." That was emphatic and he must have sensed it because he continued. "Rust Creek Falls is small and things move slower than they do in Dallas. This environment is better for my daughter."

And speaking of Wren… The little girl reversed direction and came running back to them.

"Daddy, I'm hungry."

And just like that the spell was broken. Getting to know her employer wasn't part of her job but she'd enjoyed it anyway. Hunter was so much nicer and friendlier than he'd been at first. And easy to talk to, she thought wryly. It was a little embarrassing how much she'd bared her soul, but this was a job, not a weekend getaway, and she better not forget that.

* * *

"Daddy, doesn't Merry look pretty?"

So pretty Hunter nearly swallowed his tongue. Wren and her nanny had just come out of the bedroom where they'd dressed for the wedding. Merry's dress was light purple—no, Wren would tell him that was wrong. It was lavender and left one shoulder bare, a very soft and sexy shoulder. There was an equally sexy slit in the long skirt, simple and seductive at the same time. Silky material caressed her body and made his fingers ache to touch her bare skin. He was pretty sure it made her the sexiest nanny in Rustler's Notch.

"Daddy, you look weird. Are you sick?"

"No, honey. I'm fine." He glanced at Merry with her thick wild blond hair semi-tamed, pulled back into a messy side bun. "You do look really nice."

"Thank you." Her cheeks flushed pink.

"How do I look, Daddy?" Wren spun in a circle and the full skirt of her cream-colored dress flared out.

"Like a princess."

"Do you like my dress? Merry says the style makes me look very grown-up."

"I did say that." She smiled at the little girl. "I just hope I did justice to tying that bow in the back."

"It looks good to me," he said.

"The crown of flowers in your hair is so natural and pretty, better than a tiara," Merry said.

He listened as they debated the merits of tiara versus flowers then chattered about dresses, veils, princesses and fairy tales. He loved his daughter more than anything in the world but girly stuff was way out of his comfort zone. Right up there with someday having to explain to Wren about the birds and bees.

That was a long way off, but for some reason he'd been thinking a lot about sex recently. Mostly that he hadn't had it for a long time. That was the safest reason he could come up with for last night's dreams about holding Merry in his arms. Naked.

"You look really handsome in your tuxedo, Daddy. Don't you think so, Merry?"

"Yes, he does." A becoming blush crept into her cheeks.

"Thank you, ladies. I'm glad I passed inspection. But you're the star, Wren. If you're ready, we really need to get a move on or the wedding is going to be missing a flower girl."

Fortunately they had only to go downstairs. Hunter escorted them to the bride's room, where the wedding planner was calling the shots. Merry was going to stay with Wren until just before this shindig got rolling. He proceeded to the event venue, where chairs were set up in two sections to create an aisle and there were so many flowers it looked and smelled like a garden.

Hunter had received his instructions—family and friends of the bride on the left. Groom's on the right. Logistics like this he could handle. It kept him too busy to think about Wren and whether or not she was okay. Before long most of the seats were filled, except those reserved for family in the first two rows.

Then he saw Merry walk in and his heart skipped a beat. She looked so beautiful that for a moment it was difficult to get air into his lungs. When he could breathe again, he moved toward her before any of the other ushers could.

"Hi. How's everything going?"

"Don't worry, your daughter is fine."

"Am I that transparent?" he asked.

"Yes, and good for you being a concerned father. She is so excited. And safe," she added.

"Okay." He held out his arm. "Then I will show you to your seat."

She smiled and put her hand into the bend of his elbow. "Thanks."

He led her up the aisle on the right and indicated she should sit in the front row. "Here you go."

There was surprise in her eyes. "But this is for your family."

"Wren needs to see you. In case she's nervous."

"Right. She might be a little shy with so many people watching her. Okay, then, if you think it's all right."

When she sat and demurely rearranged that silky skirt to cover her legs, Hunter sighed with disappointment. That's when he knew for sure he was going to hell for having inappropriate, sexy thoughts about the nanny.

He made one more trip to the rear of the room and received instructions to take his seat. His brothers and their wives were in place and it didn't bum him out that the chair beside Merry was empty. When he claimed it, things started to happen. Finn walked in accompanied by Max, who was his best man. He'd chosen his father for the job in the spirit of a new understanding between them. And because he didn't want to choose one of his brothers over another. The minister took his place and then the music started. Everyone stood and looked at the back of the room to get the first glimpse of the bride.

Wren was the first one down the aisle and expertly sprinkled rose petals from the basket she carried onto the white runner. She was followed by a bridesmaid in a dress the same color as the coral bow on his daughter's dress. Then he saw the bride, beautiful in a full-skirted satin dress with lacy sleeves. A veil covered her face and she was accompanied by her father, Oscar Ellington.

Hunter looked at his father and brother and saw tension on their faces. He didn't have to guess what they were thinking. His brothers looked the same way and he figured they were all wondering the same thing he was. Would there be fireworks between the bride's father and the groom's? At the rehearsal dinner last night the two men had avoided each other but they were face to face now.

"What's wrong?" Merry asked. "Your father suddenly looks like his shoes are too tight."

So she'd noticed, too. He leaned over and whispered, "Years ago he was working on a business deal with Avery's father. It went bad and Oscar is still holding a grudge."

Her eyes widened. "Surely he wouldn't do anything to spoil his daughter's wedding."

"We're about to find out."

Father and daughter stopped in front of the minister, who said, "If anyone knows why this man and this woman should not be joined in matrimony, speak now or forever hold your peace."

Hunter didn't miss the warning look Avery gave her father and without a word he lifted her veil and kissed her cheek, then gave his daughter's hand to her groom. It seemed as if there was a collective release of tension in the room and the vows went off without a hitch. Beside him Merry pulled a tissue from her small beaded purse and dabbed at her eyes.

When the ceremony was over, there were family pictures while guests moved into the room next door for the reception. Hunter was at the head table with the rest of his family for dinner and wedding toasts. Again Oscar stood and was the center of attention as well as a source of apprehension. The older man hesitated before speaking, long enough to make the Crawfords wonder if the revenge tirade was coming now.

It didn't. The man was simply gathering his emotions, and he held up a glass of champagne as he wished his daughter every happiness. Hunter couldn't imagine giving away his little girl to the son of a sworn enemy, but to his credit, Ellington did just that. Merry had been right about him not spoiling Avery's special day.

His gaze kept straying to Merry and he was impressed by her ability to chat with people at her table even as she continuously watched Wren. After dinner, when music and dancing started, keeping his daughter under surveillance became even more of a challenge. He was relieved that another pair of eyes was dedicated to that mission. Still, he picked out a discreet place to stand and watch over her.

As if living up to her name, she was flitting and flying all over the room. Right now she was dancing with the bride and groom. The three were laughing one minute and talking seriously the next. Even from this far away he could see his daughter's interest in the conversation and wondered what it was about.

A wave of melancholy washed over him as he thought how much his daughter looked like her mother. Wren was so wonderful and it made him sad that Lara wasn't here to see. And he blamed himself for that.

The dance floor was crowded but he spotted his family—Logan with Sarah, Xander and Lily, Knox holding his Genevieve. They all looked really happy. He was glad for them, but envy brought back the melancholy and with it some anger.

"Daddy?"

"Hey, kiddo." He'd been so lost in thought she'd sneaked up on him. "Are you having fun?"

"Yes." She clapped her hands together. "This is the best wedding ever."

That was a matter of opinion. He couldn't wait for it to be over. "I'm glad you're having a good time."

"I really am." She looked up at him, concern on her little face. "Are you?"

"Sure," he lied. A falsehood was okay when it was about not spoiling your child's experience, right? "This is fun."

"You don't like it," she accused.

"No?" Since when did she get so observant. "I really do. Like you said, best wedding ever."

"Then why do you look so mad and sad at the same time?" she asked.

Damn. He'd been so sure his feelings didn't show. "Do I?"

"Yes. And you're all by yourself. It's dark over here."

He glanced around the room, at the tables with their flameless candles and the flowers everywhere. There was a three-tiered cake garnished with roses on a separate table. Hanging over the dance area was a crystal chandelier that bathed the guests in a magical glow. The venue was bright and festive but he had instinctively gravitated to the darkest shadows in the room. It didn't take a shrink to tell him he was instinctively hiding from this celebration of love because it was a reminder of everything he'd lost.

"I like watching everyone dance and this is the best place to do that." He hoped that would satisfy her.

"Then why do you still look sad?"

So much for her letting this go. "I'm fine, honey. I haven't seen you dance with Gramps yet."

"I know. He's asking all the ladies to dance."

Hunter easily spotted his silver-haired father waltzing with an attractive brunette. "Yeah. He does that."

"So does Uncle Wilder."

"Yeah." His brother was living up to his name, as usual.

"I have an idea." Wren met his gaze and hers was full of earnestness.

"I know what you're going to say." He

grinned at her. "And I should have thought of it myself. You and I should have a dance."

"No."

"What?"

"You should ask Merry to dance. That would cheer you up."

While trying to figure out how to explain that Merry was an employee, Hunter looked over at her. Just then a good-looking man approached the table where she was sitting and held out his hand. Obviously an invitation to dance. Just like that he wasn't sad anymore. The new feeling was a little unfamiliar, something he hadn't experienced for a long time. It was also inconvenient and seemed to put a crack in the wall of isolation he'd spent the last six years building.

He was jealous.

Chapter Four

Since Hunter's daughter fulfilled her flower girl duties a few hours ago, Merry had barely taken her eyes off the little girl. So it didn't escape her notice when father and daughter were talking so seriously about something. Then suddenly he was looking at *her*.

"Excuse me, would you like to dance?"

Merry blinked up at the nice-looking stranger who was holding out his hand. Wren was with her dad right now so there was no reason to decline the invitation. And every reason to accept and distract herself from the way her boss's intense scrutiny was making every nerve ending in her body tingle with awareness.

"Yes. Thank you." She smiled at the patiently waiting man, then stood up and let him lead her to the dance floor, reminding herself that the toes of her too-big shoes were stuffed with tissues. "I'm Merry."

"Really?" He slid his arm around her waist and took her hand. "I've been watching and you don't look like you're having much fun."

"Oh—" She laughed. "That's my name. Meredith, but everyone calls me Merry."

"Right." His smile was self-deprecating. "My name is Don."

"Nice to meet you. And I should confess that I'm actually not a guest—"

"May I cut in?" Wilder Crawford tapped Don on the shoulder and the man shrugged before giving way. Hunter's brother took her in his arms with a grin that was a little wicked, a lot charming. "Hello, Nanny Merry."

"Good Lord, that makes me sound like I'm a hundred years old."

"You sure don't look it. Not in that dress."

His appraisal was flirty and full of male appreciation, both of which she took as a compliment and nothing more. "Well, I am being paid to supervise your niece, who's with her father at the moment. And that's the only reason I accepted an offer to dance with that man. And you, by the way."

"Why do I feel as if I've just been rapped on the knuckles with a ruler?" His dark eyes glowed with mischief.

"That could have something to do with my working in elementary education. It's my job to keep children under control."

His eyebrows rose. "I'm sensing some disapproval."

"No. Not judging, just observing," she protested. "And it didn't escape my notice that you have danced with many women here at the reception."

"I didn't want anyone to feel left out." His roguish expression intensified.

"So you were being unselfish? It wasn't a

screening process to find someone for the evening?"

That surprised him. "I'm sorry, what?"

"It's a well-known fact that at weddings there's that one groomsman who is looking for a hookup—"

"I'm cutting in." Hunter tapped his brother on the shoulder with a little more enthusiasm than seemed necessary.

Wilder looked the tiniest bit relieved when he let her go to his brother. "I hope you can handle her better than me, big brother."

Hunter stared at his brother's back as he weaved his way through the dancers on the way to the bar. "What does that mean?"

"I don't think he's used to being challenged. My guess is that women line up around the block or pick a number if there's a chance to get his attention."

Hunter's eyes glittered with intensity as he took her hand in his and slid his arm around her waist, leading her into a waltz. "Did he come on to you?"

"No. He was flirty, that's all. I think the behavior is hardwired into him." The youngest Crawford was very handsome, and clearly he liked women. But she wasn't the least bit tempted by him. On the other hand, the man holding her was temptation with a capital *T.* "I accused him of being that guy trolling for a woman."

He stopped moving for a moment and met her gaze. "So you called him on his crap."

"I just made an observation. And explained that every wedding has at least one grooms-man who makes it his mission to sleep with a bridesmaid or one of the guests."

"You don't pull any punches. No won-der he headed for the bar." Hunter's mouth curved up at the corners. "So, he wasn't too forward?"

"I was the forward one and probably shouldn't have said anything. I think I shocked him. He was a perfect gentleman." She glanced around and spotted Wren danc-ing with her grandfather. Then she stumbled and stepped on Hunter's foot, the unfortunate consequence of wearing shoes that were too big. "Sorry."

"No problem. And I'm glad he behaved himself."

"I've noticed that between Wilder and your father, single women of all ages are receiving a lot of attention tonight." She smiled up at him. "You're going to have to step up your game big-time to keep pace with the Crawford bachelors."

That remark could go either way but her responsibilities were nearly over. So she didn't really have much to lose.

Unexpectedly, Hunter smiled and his somber seriousness fell away as if a magic spell had transformed the beast back into a handsome prince. And handsome was the operative word. She'd seen him in jeans, boots, Stetson—and the cowboy look made her female parts tingle. But there was something indescribable and luscious about a man in a tuxedo.

Especially a man like this one. The black jacket, pants and bow tie made him look dashing, but the way the starched white shirt contrasted with his tanned skin took her breath away. He was absolutely irresistible and the realization made her trip again and nearly lose a shoe.

"Sorry," she muttered.

"I hardly noticed what with my curiosity about being designated an endangered species. One of the last three Crawford bachelors." Then his smile faded. "Although it's hard to think of my dad like that since he was married. And divorced."

"Everyone in town is talking about him paying Vivienne Dalton to find wives for his sons. Is that rumor true?" Merry asked.

"Yes."

When he settled their joined hands on his chest, she forgot to clench her toes to keep her shoes on and walked right out of one. She would have toppled over without his arms around her.

She sighed. "I have a confession."

"Those are not words any man wants to hear."

"Well, it's not something I'm particularly thrilled to tell you, but it's better than leaving you with the impression that I'm a hopeless klutz." She held on to his arm while sliding her shoe back on. "I borrowed this outfit from a friend. The shoes match but her feet are bigger than mine. I have to admit when I came to interview for this job I wasn't expecting to dance."

He looked relieved. "Is that all."

Speaking of which, she gazed past him and found his daughter hanging with her uncle Logan, aunt Sarah and their baby daughter, Sophia. Wren seemed in awe of the baby.

Merry was about to go back to her table but another slow song started and Hunter put his strong arms around her again. He was barely moving his feet, allowing her to barely move hers. That kept her shoes firmly in place.

"Problem solved," he said against her hair.

Merry's mouth went dry. Their bodies were touching now from chest to knee because he was holding her more securely. But that was about shoe integrity, not because he was enjoying the closeness as much as she was.

"So," she said, feeling an overwhelming need to break the charged silence. "About your father. Max doesn't look a lot like Cupid, but what he's doing, I mean trying to fix you all up, is actually very sweet."

"You wouldn't say that if the pressure was on you," he said. "Women might throw themselves at Wilder, but my dad is throwing them at both of us."

"Since we're dancing at the wedding of his fourth successful match, it would seem something he's doing is working," she pointed out. "Is it possible he just wants you to be happy?"

"That's a hard maybe. He's into control, when not wrapped up in himself."

"Parents aren't perfect, Hunter."

His look was wry. "That doesn't bode well for me."

"I'm simply stating a fact. By definition, human beings are flawed. That doesn't mean you don't try. All anyone can do is their best." She looked up at him. "When my mom died, my dad became distant and withdrawn. As an adult I understand that he was grieving, but back then… I just felt alone."

"It can't have been easy for him."

The shadows in Hunter's eyes reminded her of how her father had looked when remembering her mom. Merry would bet almost anything that Hunter was thinking about losing his wife.

"No, it wasn't easy. It took time, but eventually we became close. He never said anything, but I always had the feeling he was doing his best to make up for shutting me out."

Hunter shook his head. "You don't know my dad. He makes no apologies, and fixing us up is nothing more than a power trip."

"Daddy!" Wren ran over to them and looked up, grinning from ear to ear. "You and Merry are dancing, just like the prince and Cinderella did in my favorite movie.

Are you going to kiss Merry like the prince kissed her at the end when they got married?"

There must be some kind of weird cosmic rule about having almost total silence in a crowded room when something completely embarrassing was said. Merry was pretty sure the child's words could be heard all the way to Rust Creek Falls. Around them dancers stopped and stared and her cheeks grew hot with humiliation.

Hunter went down on one knee in front of his daughter. "Honey, that's not something you should ask."

"Why?"

"It's personal and Merry works for me."

"But you stopped dancin'."

"Because of my shoes," Merry said.

Hunter held his daughter's hand and led her to the side of the dance floor. "Merry is my employee and that would be inappropriate. Do you know what that means?"

"I'm six, Daddy." Her voice was tinged with irritation.

"I know. It means that doing anything personal—"

"Like kissin' her?"

"Yes, like that." Hunter blew out a long breath. "It would make her feel awkward and I would never do that to her."

"But you looked like you were going to. I don't get why—" Tears glistened in her eyes and then she started to cry.

He gathered her into his arms then looked helplessly up at Merry.

"Maybe it's time to go upstairs and chill," she suggested. "This little girl has been going a mile a minute all day and I think she's just exhausted. What do you say, sweetie?"

Wren wiped tears from her face. "Yes."

"Okay."

She held out her hand and the little girl put hers into Merry's palm. "I'll get my purse. My room key is in there."

As the two of them moved toward the table, Merry walked right out of her shoe. And, embarrassing cosmic rule number two, everyone was still staring at them.

Wren stopped and looked up at her. "You lost your shoe at the ball. Just like Cinderella."

"Yeah." But not exactly. The handsome prince wasn't coming after her.

She slid her foot back into the shoe and hurried them both out of the ballroom, leaving Hunter behind. She'd been hired so that he could have a good time at the wedding. And, as Wilder Crawford had pointed out, there was no shortage of ladies for him to have a good time with.

It wasn't in her job description to hate that, but she did anyway.

"Seems as if everyone's having a good time."

Hunter was forced to look at his father and away from the door where Merry had disappeared with his daughter. He'd moved from the dance floor to the bar, where he was watching the other guests milling around, dancing and sitting at tables. It was impossible to miss the bride all in white and her groom holding tightly to her hand. They looked really happy and for some reason that made him unreasonably angry because he realized Merry had taken all the fun with her.

"Yeah."

"Great party, if I do say so myself." Max's tone was full of self-congratulation, but that was nothing new.

"This is Finn and Avery's doing since it was their idea to get remarried in front of their families."

"It was my doing to fly everyone in and make sure there was high-end champagne for the toasts. And people are having fun. I even saw you out there dancing."

That was a mistake, Hunter thought. Merry Matthews had felt way too good in his arms. Her sweet curves fit perfectly against him and she smelled like flowers, just the way a woman should. He could have gone the rest of his life and been just fine without knowing that and now he had to find a way to forget how good she smelled.

"Did you hear me, son?"

Crap. He looked up at Max. "Hmm?"

"I said, my little granddaughter sure picked herself a fetching nanny."

Hunter wondered if that was a criticism or a warning, a reminder that starting something with the hired help was a slippery slope. Twenty-four hours from now she wouldn't be his employee. He wasn't sure whether that was good or bad and took his annoyance out on the handiest target.

"Seriously, Dad? Fetching? What is this? The Middle Ages?"

"What can I say?" Max grinned, looking every inch the silver fox. "I'm a Renaissance man."

"Right."

A romantic ballad started playing and Finn led his bride to the center of the dance floor then tucked her against him. She slid her arms around his neck and they seemed to be in their own world. Hunter had dipped a toe into that world just a little while ago. And then Wren said what she said and he went into damage control mode.

The thing was, he'd been thinking about kissing Merry. He was holding her and she looked so damn cute confessing about her borrowed shoes being too big. Touching his mouth to hers felt like the next step, the most natural thing in the world. He was almost glad Wren interrupted. Although it would have been better if she'd used her indoor voice and not the one astronauts on the space station could hear.

"Where's your brother?" Max asked.

"Which one? I have five."

"Smart-ass." His dad laughed. "I was talk-ing about Wilder. Haven't seen him since you cut in on his dance with Merry. Where do you suppose he is?"

Probably somewhere private hooking up with a woman. Remembering Merry ex-plaining the concept made Hunter smile. "Maybe he just went to get some air."

"Doubtful." Max shook his head.

"And isn't he the one who promised to help

keep an eye on Wren so that I could loosen up?" he asked wryly.

"One and the same," his father agreed. "It would appear that my suggestion to hire a nanny has worked out well. In more ways than one."

Hunter refused to get sucked in and ask what he meant by that. "My daughter picked her own nanny."

"My granddaughter is an excellent judge of people. Just like her gramps." Max clapped a hand on his son's shoulder as he scanned the guests. His gaze settled on one in particular. "And I judge that right over there is a very fetching woman sitting all by herself who might like to dance."

"Go for it, Dad."

Turning serious, his father met his gaze. "I could say the same thing to you. There are more than a few women here who could use a healthy dose of Crawford charm. Since Wilder is missing in action, that leaves you and me to uphold the family honor and reputation."

"I'm right behind you." Not.

After his father moved away, Hunter ordered a whiskey neat from the bar and watched all the guests still celebrating. His four brothers and their wives were in a group, talking, laughing, carefree and happy in a way he never would be again. Not for the first time he felt as if he was on the outside looking in. Until moving to Rust Creek Falls, the bond of brotherhood had remained strong, the circle tight. But that was changing, and he truly wished them every happiness, at the same time feeling sorry for himself that they were leaving him behind.

Man, was this pathetic, he thought. His daughter was upstairs in her room and she was his whole world. That's where he should be. So he tossed back the rest of his drink and took his pity party on the road, quietly slipping out of the ballroom. The elevators were like a ghost town and he made it to his floor quickly, then quietly let himself into the suite.

The lights were on and he noticed that

Merry's door was wide open but the room was dark. He crossed to where Wren was supposed to be sleeping and found her still awake.

"Hi, Daddy. I'm glad you're here."

"Why aren't you asleep?" He turned on her light, then sat at the foot of her bed. "I thought you were tired."

"I am," she said. "I closed my eyes while Merry read me a story and tucked me in. But my eyes wouldn't stay shut."

"Do you want me to read you another story?"

"No." She sat up. "I'm hungry."

"Didn't you eat at the reception?"

"Cake. I didn't like any of the other stuff. Gross," she said making a face.

If it wasn't chicken nuggets and fries she turned up her nose. Come to think of it, nothing on the wedding menu was kid friendly. So a sugar buzz explained the meltdown and insomnia.

"Okay, kid, let's see if that mini-bar in the other room has something that meets with your approval." Her smile and enthusiastic nod made him grin. "And we have a plan."

She put on her fuzzy pink robe and matching slippers and they raided the snacks that would cost Max an arm and a leg. Served him right, Hunter thought with a smile of satisfaction.

He brought the basket containing nuts, crackers and trail mix over to the sofa, then opened a bottle of bubbly water and poured some into a tumbler and put it on a coffee table coaster.

"Can I have soda?" she asked hopefully.

"No. I'm giving you a moratorium on sugar."

"What's that?" There was a puzzled look on her little face.

"It's like a time-out." He sat beside her and opened the can of nuts.

"Oh." She looked up at him. "Maybe Merry is hungry, too."

There hadn't been a sound from her room since he'd come in. She'd probably left her door open in order to hear if Wren needed anything. "She's asleep. Let's not disturb her."

If only he could say she hadn't disturbed him. She'd been one big disturbance since he'd seen her in that lavender dress and he needed some space to get back his perspective. Talking with his daughter should do it.

"Did you have fun tonight?" he asked her.

"It was the best wedding ever."

"How many have you been to?" He knew the answer was zero. Four of his brothers were married now but this had been the only big event. Thanks in part to their father, it had been a good one.

"Only one," she admitted, "but it was the best. I love my dress."

"There will be lots of pictures for you to remember everything, including how special you looked in that dress." He knew rehashing the event would settle her down so she could get some rest. "What else did you like?"

Thoughtful, she chewed a peanut. "I'm

glad Merry was here. Didn't she look pretty, Daddy?"

A vision of slender curves and that sexy slit in the lavender material flashed through his mind, stunning his body as surely as if he'd been sucker punched. "She did look pretty."

"I don't know if there are any pictures of her." Wren frowned.

"The photographer was all over the place. I bet there are a lot of shots with Merry in them."

"Maybe they're of you and Merry dancing." She looked up at him, her face impossibly young, her expression achingly hopeful. "Didn't you like dancing with her? You didn't look sad when you were."

Between controlling the urge to kiss Merry and enjoying the feel of her in his arms, there hadn't been time to be sad. But his emotional quotient was not what was on Wren's mind. And he would have to be an idiot not to see that his daughter was trying to hook him up with her nanny. He slid his arm along the back of the sofa as an overwhelming need to hold and protect his little girl knotted inside him.

"Look, honey, I get that you want Merry and me to—"

"She could be your girlfriend," Wren supplied.

"No, honey—"

"But, Daddy, she was like Cinderella when you were dancing. She lost her shoe. And you helped her. Like Prince Charming. In the story they were in love," she said hopefully.

"But that's a fairy tale. She can't be my girlfriend."

"But why?"

"There are a lot of reasons," he said.

"I hate that you always have reasons." Her look challenged him to make a list.

"It's just not as easy as that." In spite of what his father thought about setting his sons up. "Just because someone wants you to like someone as a girlfriend doesn't mean they will."

"Why not?"

"Well, when a man and woman meet, there needs to be an attraction."

"Like you think someone is pretty."

"Right."

"You said Merry looked pretty tonight. Are you 'tracted?"

Try another way to explain this, he thought. "It's more than just how someone looks. It's about talking to them."

"I saw you talkin' to Merry. You laughed," his observant daughter pointed out.

He couldn't say she was wrong about that. The fact that Merry had called Wilder on his crap seemed so at odds with her innocence that it had surprised a chuckle out of him.

"It's more complicated than that, honey. Merry works for me and it's not right to make her feel uncomfortable."

"After tomorrow she won't be my nanny anymore." There was a wistful tone in her voice.

He'd thought the same thing a little while ago and was conflicted about it. Time for a change of subject. "So, what was your favorite thing about the wedding? Other than your dress."

"Dancing with Uncle Finn and Aunt Avery."

"Okay. Why?" he asked.

"They told me about a diary."

Hunter didn't have to ask what she meant. After buying the Ambling A and moving in, they'd found a leather-bound, jewel-encrusted book underneath a loose floorboard at the main house. Nate Crawford made the connection to the Abernathys, who'd previously owned the ranch, and they'd been doing research on the family. So far no information had turned up. As each of his brothers got married, the brothers had slipped the diary into their wedding-night luggage, claiming what was written inside was passionate and romantic. He was skeptical. And he hoped that his brother and sister-in-law had enough sense not to fill Wren's head with weird, woo-woo stuff.

"What did they say about the diary?"

"That whoever wrote in it didn't get a happy ending," she said.

"That's too bad, honey. But not everyone does."

"Well, they should," she said stubbornly. "Especially you, Daddy. Because Mommy died. But I don't think she would want you always to be sad. You looked happy with Merry. If you were together, you wouldn't be sad anymore."

Out of the mouths of babes… Wren was everything to him, but there'd been an emptiness inside him for the last six years after losing her mom. "Life isn't a fairy tale, sweetie."

"I know." Her tone was sulky and her look could fry eggs. "If it was, the whole family could live together in a castle. I wouldn't have to miss having my aunts around."

"Your aunt Gen and uncle Knox live in one of the other cabins. She's around."

"But she's always working with the horses. And Aunt Avery and Uncle Finn are moving up to that old hunting cabin so they can be alone. No one is there for me." She glared up at him as if this was somehow his fault. "And especially Merry. I like her here. She makes everything more fun, just like she does at school."

"I didn't know you felt that way."

"I'm the only girl around, Daddy." She crawled into his lap and rested her head on his shoulder. "It's always only Gramps and Uncle Wilder and you."

"Thanks for telling me this." And throwing a monkey wrench into everything.

It was sobering to realize that he couldn't be everything to her. By sheer numbers he'd thought he, his dad and brothers had all the bases covered in raising this little girl. He couldn't have been more wrong. And she was getting older. Maybe it would be a good thing to have more of a female presence in her life.

To keep this child happy, he would walk on hot coals. And what he was considering definitely fell under the heading of "into the fire."

Chapter Five

Merry never had hotel room service before. And coffee, orange juice, waffles and eggs brought on a cart and served by a waiter should have lifted her mood after the conversation she'd overheard last night. It didn't. The door to her room had been wide open so she could hear if Wren needed her. The bedside lamp had been off, but she'd been awake, looking at the stars from her window. There had probably still been some in her eyes after dancing with the handsome rancher.

She'd thought there was a connection and

had felt a little like the Cinderella Wren talked about. But it seemed Prince Charming had no interest in love. He'd fallen back on the employer/employee dynamic even though in a few hours the work relationship would be over. There could be something if he wanted there to be. Obviously she was the only one with a crush.

Everything Hunter had said was the truth, and it shouldn't hurt, but for some reason it did. Maybe because now she was going back to her regularly scheduled life. With all its problems. So now she was packing her bags. This trip had been magical in some ways, not so much in others, and it was all but over.

She zipped up her suitcase and wheeled it into the suite's living room. Then she walked to Wren's room and poked her head in. The little girl was wadding up her clothes and throwing them into her pink princess bag.

"Would you like some help?"

Wren turned and there were tears in her eyes. "Oh, Merry, it's—"

"What is it, sweetie?" She moved closer,

sat on the bed and gathered the child into her lap, holding her tight. "What's wrong, love?"

"We're going home." The words were hard to understand between sobs.

"I know. It's hard going back after having so much fun. But you can't be on vacation forever."

"It's not that." She burrowed in.

"Then what?" Merry pressed a hand to the child's forehead. "Do you feel all right?"

"Yes. I'm just sad."

"Do you want to talk about it? Maybe I can help."

"You can't. I'm cryin' because now I'll only be able to see you at school. You won't be there when I wake up in the morning or at night when I go to sleep."

She snuggled the child closer, trying to offer comfort. Wren had pushed Merry at her father last night and he wasn't having it. He was closed off and not even the daughter he loved more than anything could convince him to change his mind. Her heart hurt for both father and daughter.

From the corner of her eye she saw movement and noticed Hunter standing in the doorway. She wasn't sure how long he'd been there or what he'd heard.

"You okay, Wren?" he asked.

"Fine." The tearful tone was dripping with drama and emotion. It didn't take a mental giant to see that she was telling him what he wanted to hear.

"Do you want to talk about it?"

"No." She sat up and glared at him.

He looked as if he might push back, then didn't. "Okay. Finish packing, then I'll get a bellman for the luggage. The cars will be here soon to take us to the airport."

"I don't want to go. Cuz I'll have to say goodbye to Aunt Sarah, Aunt Lily, Aunt Genevieve and Aunt Avery."

"I know things are changing. Aunt Lily and Uncle Xander have moved to their own ranch house. Aunt Sarah and Uncle Logan live in town. You can visit them. They fixed up her parents' house and you can visit baby Sophia."

"It's not the same," she said stubbornly.

"You'll see them all again soon. The whole family will be together for Thanksgiving in a couple of weeks."

"It will never be the same again. But I know we have to go." She sniffled then gave Merry a hug. Without another word she slid to the floor and put her nightgown in the suitcase.

"I've got this," Merry told him.

"Okay."

He looked relieved and possibly eager to be off the hook. Poor guy. She felt sorry for him. His daughter was growing up and girls were kind of a mystery to men. Her own father had told her that more than once.

Merry looked at Wren. "I'll check the drawers and make sure you have everything."

"Okay."

Forty-five minutes later those cars Hunter had mentioned unloaded the Crawford family and Merry not far from the jet waiting to take them home to Rust Creek Falls. As the group assembled, Merry looked around and frowned. In the last couple of days she'd sort of gotten used to counting Crawford heads. When your job involved keeping track of five- and six-year-olds, ticking off a list in your mind became second nature. So she noticed that three members were not present and accounted for.

"Wait. Finn and Avery aren't here."

Max happened to be next to her. "They're staying here for a few days."

"Right." Merry shaded her eyes with her hand as she looked up at him and was blinded by the sun. "Their honeymoon."

"Yeah."

He was grinning from ear to ear, but Merry didn't think it was "that's my boy" or "chip off the old block" stuff. The man seemed genuinely pleased that his son was married, happy and the family celebration had gone off without a hitch. However, there might be a hitch in the ride home since one more of them was missing.

"Wilder's not here either. Is he staying for the honeymoon, too?" she asked wryly.

Max's smile slipped. "Finn would have something to say about that. No. He texted and said he would meet us here. And before you ask, he didn't stay in his room at the resort."

Merry wasn't sure why he was confiding this information to her and was reluctant to comment the way she had to Hunter. "I wasn't prying. It's just habit. At the school one of the things they pay me for is to make sure everyone is where they should be."

His glance settled on Wren who was soaking up attention from her three aunts while she still could. Then Max looked at Merry. "I want to thank you for taking care of my granddaughter this weekend. She seems to like you very much and that goes a long way with me."

"She's a very special little girl. It's impossible not to fall in love with her."

"I couldn't agree more." A car pulled up

behind the SUVs and Wilder got out. "Seems the prodigal son has arrived."

"That completes the head count."

"Thank you again, Merry." He gave her a quick bear hug. "Excuse me. I have to herd everyone on board."

Merry wasn't the last one to get on the plane, but the seating area in the front section was pretty full. Wren was there with her aunts and uncles so she picked a bench seat in the rear by herself. After all, she was only the hired help.

Moments after she was settled, the stragglers boarded. Hunter was the last and he looked around, then hesitated only a moment before sitting beside her. He didn't say anything so she didn't either. *Let it be awkward,* she thought.

The announcement was made to buckle up and the flight attendant secured the cabin for takeoff. It wasn't long before they were airborne.

Hunter cleared his throat. "I have a check for you."

"It doesn't seem right to take money. Looking after Wren isn't work, and a stay at that fabulous resort was wonderful. A lovely break from my routine."

"Still, I hired you to make sure she was well looked after and she was. So, here."

She looked at the piece of paper he held out. "My employment is officially complete."

"Yeah."

She took it and tucked the check into her wallet. "Thank you."

"You're welcome."

Merry studied his expression and guessed that he was uneasy. "Was there something else?"

"Yeah."

"I thought so."

"Why?" He sounded surprised.

"Because there are other seats open and you sat next to me. I figured it was to talk." Because she knew he wasn't attracted to her. "I hope you were satisfied with the supervision I provided Wren."

"I was. But more important, she was happy."

Hunter glanced away for a moment and took a deep breath. "I heard what she said to you earlier. When she was packing."

Merry didn't know what to say to that except, "I didn't put her up to that."

"The thought never crossed my mind."

She nodded. "I wouldn't worry. She's probably just tired. It was a busy weekend."

"And she was up late last night."

Merry was aware of that fact but didn't confirm she knew. It was best he didn't know she'd overheard that particular conversation. "She'll be fine once she's home."

"Will she?"

Merry's gaze snapped to his. "Why wouldn't she be?"

"For one thing, she's become very attached to you."

"And, like I told her, she will see me at school. This weekend hasn't changed anything." That was a lie. After dancing with Hunter, aka Prince Charming, she'd changed. But real life would get her over it. "Going back to her routine will fix whatever is bothering her."

"Maybe that's not enough." He looked lost. "It's possible she needs more female influence in her life. Last night she said some things—"

"Oh?" she said innocently.

His expression was intense. "The words don't matter. I just don't want her to ever think I didn't listen to her. So—"

"What?"

"I'd like to hire you to be Wren's nanny. It will be a full-time, live-in job."

She hadn't seen that coming and was on the verge of turning him down until he told her the salary he had in mind. Still, she said, "I already have a job at the school."

"The way I see it, there's no reason to quit since you both have the same schedule. You could take her and bring her home. That frees me up for ranch work because you'll be with her."

"Wow, I—" Her mind was racing. She'd literally just been thinking how meeting him had changed her but going home would get her over it. The intense attraction was a very good reason for her to say no.

But she couldn't ignore the fact that accepting the offer would solve two of her most pressing problems—money and a place to live when the house sold. She would be a fool to pass up this opportunity.

"In that case, thank you. I would love to be Wren's nanny."

And if there was a God in heaven, Hunter would never suspect how she felt about him.

The first day back from the wedding was Hunter's first day to wonder what he'd been thinking to hire Merry Matthews to be the live-in nanny. She'd brought Wren home from school then unpacked her own things in one of the cabin's two extra upstairs bedrooms.

Merry had the table set when he came in from working and she greeted him with a sunny smile, a beer and the best meatloaf and mashed potatoes he'd ever tasted. Somehow she'd even flimflammed his daughter into eating her green beans without an argument. So, his problem with Merry had nothing to do with her work and everything to do with his attraction to her.

Now he was alone downstairs while happy noises and laughter drifted to him from the second floor. At the wedding he'd seen how content his married brothers were and he felt like he was on the outside looking in. He'd never expected to feel that way in his own home. It was always him and Wren against the world, but now Merry was here making meatloaf and supervising his child's bath.

He was too restless to watch TV and decided to make sure Merry knew where the soap and towels were kept. At the top of the stairs the master bedroom was on his left. He turned the other way and passed his daughter's room, then stopped. The bathroom door was open and the little girl was standing in front of the oak-framed oval mirror and wearing her favorite pink nightgown. Merry was behind her, combing her hair.

"Hi, Daddy."

"Hey, kiddo. I can't believe you're clean already."

"Merry said if I was fast there would be time before bed to show me how to French braid my hair."

"Did she now?"

"She did," Merry confirmed. "I'm a solid believer in the carrot-and-stick method of negotiation. Better known as rewarding positive behavior."

"And you have the positive results to back you up." He leaned a shoulder against the doorjamb.

"I do. She lived up to her end of the bargain so now I have to pay up." She smiled into the mirror. "So what'll it be, sweetie? Braids? Pigtails?" She gathered the wet strands that lightened to golden blond when dry and pulled them up to the crown of Wren's head. "Top knot?"

"French braids. I already told you."

"Just making sure you haven't changed your mind."

It hadn't taken Merry long to figure out that this child often altered the plan when he thought she'd set her heart on something. Sometimes Wren made his head spin but this woman seemed to take it in stride. Points to her.

"Daddy doesn't know how to French braid," Wren teased. "He can only do a ponytail."

"I'm sure he has other very important skills."

He thought for a moment. "As a matter of fact, I fixed the door on your dollhouse. Remember?"

"Is that true?" Merry's hands stilled as she met the child's gaze in the mirror.

"Yes, ma'am." She nodded enthusiastically and nearly pulled her hair from the nanny's loose grip. "He made it for me, too."

"That big beautiful wooden Victorian dollhouse with the lovely details? The one taking up a large portion of her room. You built that?" Her eyes were wide and full of amazement.

"With my bare hands." He swore he could

almost feel his chest puffing out because he'd impressed her.

"Where were you when I was a little girl?"

"Probably a little boy dipping a little girl's French braid in the inkwell."

She laughed. "Actually that was a rhetorical question. But seriously, it's a beautiful job. I would have loved something like that when I was a child." She looked at Wren. "Your dad can't do hair but you're very fortunate that he has some serious dollhouse skills."

"Thank you, Daddy."

"You're welcome."

"That reminds me," Wren said. "In school today we made a turkey out of construction paper. My teacher was tellin' us about the very first Thanksgiving."

"Yeah?" Merry secured the braid she just finished.

"Yes. And she said the holiday will be here before we know it."

"That's true." He was only half listening

because the concentration on Merry's face as she worked was so darn cute.

"We're having a first Thanksgiving, too. Just like the pilgrims."

"You are?" Merry said.

"Uh-huh." Again Wren nodded and this time did pull her hair out of the nanny's hands. She had to start over. "Sorry."

"No problem. Please continue."

"This will be Daddy's and my first Thanksgiving here on the ranch."

"Wow. That's exciting." Her tone was bright and shiny, but her expression didn't match. There was sadness in her eyes. "Sometimes firsts are fun and sometimes they're not."

"You'll be missing your dad this year," Hunter guessed.

She glanced at him and nodded. "This is my first one without him. Ever."

"I'm sorry, Merry," the little girl said. "I never had Thanksgiving with my mom because she died when I was a baby."

Hunter noticed that his daughter had dropped the "Miss" when she talked to Merry. The little girl was clearly comfortable with her new nanny. He remembered that first Thanksgiving without Lara and whatever the definition of fun was, that holiday didn't even come close. He'd been knee-deep in diapers, formula and sleepless nights. But if it hadn't been for Wren and his family, he didn't think he'd have gotten through that dark time at all.

"You know, sweetie, you're very lucky to have all your family close by. And not just for the holiday. Not everyone is so fortunate."

It occurred to Hunter that he didn't know a lot about her family except the little she'd shared. That she and her father had moved to Rust Creek Falls right after the flood. And she had a brother who joined the military. Was she completely alone now? He wanted to know but couldn't phrase the question like that.

"But you have a brother," Hunter said.

"Yes."

He expected her to elaborate, but she pressed her lips tightly together. No one would ever accuse him of being fluent in body language but hers clearly said she wouldn't tell him more. Of course that just made him more curious about her story. Including, now that he thought about it, was there a special man in her life? Fortunately his daughter was oblivious to the signals and didn't let the subject go.

"What's your brother's name?"

"Jack."

"Where does he live?" Wren asked.

"He's in the military. Right now he lives overseas."

"Is that far?" The little girl's eyes grew wider.

"Very far. We don't see each other much."

Hunter wasn't sure why he recognized that this separation pained her, but he did. Maybe because of his own loss, kindred spirits and all that. Still the why of it didn't matter. All he knew was that Merry wasn't living up to her name. And something told him there was more to this than just geographical distance. If eyes were the window to the soul, hers were revealing a painful bruise. Jack had somehow hurt her.

Merry secured the second braid and forced a smile. "Ta-da. You are gorgeous. Do you like it?"

Turning her head from side to side Wren said, "Yes. Can you do it like this for Thanksgiving?"

"Of course. You'll be the prettiest six-year-old at the table."

"I'll be the only one there," the little girl said.

"Really?" Merry tapped her lip thoughtfully. "That's right. Baby Sophia isn't big enough to walk yet."

"She can't talk either."

"True. Not a lot of company in your demographic," Merry sympathized.

"Does that mean I have no one to talk to?" Wren asked.

"Yes." Merry glanced at Hunter and the corners of her mouth curved up in amusement.

"Your aunts will all be there," Hunter reminded her.

"Cool."

"You're going to have a wonderful holiday," Merry said. "And you can tell me all about it."

"But you're going to be there, too," the little girl said.

"I don't know." She shrugged.

"You have to be here. With me. And my family. We can have our firsts together."

"Your first one in Montana and my first without my dad." Merry met his gaze though she spoke to Wren. "It's not up to me, sweetie."

Hunter wasn't sure how his daughter had grown into the thoughtful, caring person she was. He couldn't believe he hadn't extended the invitation already. His only excuse was being preoccupied with Merry's mouth. More specifically how her lips would feel against his own. Would they be as soft as he expected? Maybe she would taste like sunshine and fresh air.

Both of the females in the room were staring at him and for a second he was afraid he'd said that out loud.

"What?" he asked them.

"Da-ad." Wren rolled her eyes. "Is it okay for Merry to have Thanksgiving with us?"

"We can talk about this later," Merry interjected. "I don't want you to feel like you're on the spot. It's really fine. I'll have dinner with my friend Zoey—"

"It's okay. Wren wants you here and you're more than welcome. So, dinner with the Crawfords on Thanksgiving is a go. The more the Merry-er."

"Like I've never heard that one before." The nanny grinned at him then giggled with Wren.

"So will you? Come with us to Gramps's

house for Thanksgiving?" There was a note of coaxing in Wren's tone.

"I wouldn't miss it."

Wren turned and pressed herself against Merry, wrapping her small arms around her waist. "It's a good thing you're here. You have us to spend the holiday with."

"And I am so very lucky." She bent and kissed the top of the little girl's head. "And on that note, it has to be said that it's time—"

"For bed," Wren finished. Then she laughed.

Hunter couldn't believe it. No drama. Zero argument. Just good-natured surrender to the inevitable. Had he been doing something wrong? Was the nanny sprinkling rainbows and fairy dust on his child?

More important—what was he? Chopped liver?

That sounded a little bit ungrateful. It was probably just about the newness of the situation. The little girl he knew and loved couldn't keep this up for long. But contemplating that philosophical question was better than thinking about the one uppermost in his mind. Had it been a mistake to hire Merry? He had decidedly mixed feelings about her living here.

On the one hand, Wren seemed happy to have a woman here. Hence the bedtime capitulation. On the other hand, the moment Hunter came home and saw dinner ready followed by Merry offering him a beer, he'd begun to ache in places he'd been sure had died a long time ago.

He didn't want to feel again but he did, and having her here was the only difference between yesterday and today. This wasn't anything he'd anticipated and he acknowledged it might have been a major miscalculation to offer her the job. But that horse had already left the barn.

Chapter Six

Normally Hunter liked riding fences to check that the posts and wire didn't need repair or make sure a cow wasn't stuck in the fence. But this morning his father was with him. Max had insisted he wanted to come along, but surely he had an agenda. The man always did.

He glanced over and admired the way his father sat a horse, the way he'd taught Hunter and his brothers to ride. Straight, tall and proud. Maximilian Crawford was an imposing figure, but Hunter wished he was an imposing figure in his ranch office instead.

"I think you should start dating again," his father said.

"And there it is."

"What?" There was a little too much innocence in Max's gravelly voice.

"The reason you got up before God to keep me company."

"It does make you kind of a captive audience." Max grinned, completely unashamed. "I just want to talk to you about getting back in the saddle, no pun intended."

"Dating."

"Right."

"Then this will be a short conversation, Dad. I dated a little back in Dallas. I don't want to get serious. Good talk."

Max nodded, his black Stetson casting a shadow that hid his eyes. "I was also thinking about how much I like Montana. The land. The mountains. Coming here and making a change is going to be good for this family. Hell, it already is. Look how happy your brothers are."

"I agree."

Hunter had noticed, and he envied them but that was his problem. On the other hand, his daughter had never been happier since Merry had come to live with them. He still wasn't convinced hiring her was the right move because every time she walked into a room need knotted deep in his gut. She was messing with his head, had him picturing himself running his hands through all that silky blond hair and kissing her full lips. And it wasn't just his head she was messing with. The rest of his body wanted in on the action. There were so many reasons why that was a bad idea.

Hunter became aware that his father was staring at him as they clip-clopped along. "What?"

"I can't recall the last time you agreed with me about anything."

"Well, I do, about moving to Montana. Wren is settling in really well." Thanks to Merry.

And as if Max could read his mind, he

said, "Hiring Merry to be her nanny has made a difference then?"

"Seems so." It had been only a few days since she moved into the house, but they'd fallen seamlessly into a routine. And the woman was making herself indispensable to him, as well. Her being there took pressure and stress off him as far as ranch chores late at night or early in the morning. Like today.

"It doesn't hurt that we left a lot of bad memories behind in Texas," Max said.

"You're not wrong, Dad."

The ranch and city of Dallas itself had reminders everywhere Hunter went. It was where he and Lara had started their life together and where hers had ended. He'd been a grieving husband and single dad who had no clue how to care for an infant daughter.

"How did you manage it all?" he asked his father. "After Mom left, I mean."

"Badly."

Hunter rested his gloved hands on the saddle horn and glanced sideways. He'd never heard that particular tone of regret in Max's voice before. "What do you mean?"

"Your mom wanted out of the marriage, and I didn't want to let her go. Consequently I made a lot of mistakes, as a husband and a father."

"Such as?"

Max's mouth pulled tight and his body slumped a little in the saddle. The image of dejection and sadness. "She wasn't happy but I tried to force her to stay anyway. I tried to control the situation and used my own sons as leverage. That just made everything worse."

"How?" Hunter and his brothers had lived the nightmare of their mom being there one day then gone the next, and never seeing her again. But his father had never talked about this before and he needed to hear it.

"You boys didn't have a mom. I kept you from her to try and get her to come back. It backfired. And now I see the true meaning of that saying—you reap what you sow. The chickens have come home to roost."

"What do you mean? Just spit it out, Dad."

"All of you boys are reluctant to commit to love. And that's my fault."

Hunter sighed. "Correct me if I'm wrong. Four of my brothers are married. That seems an awful lot like commitment to me."

"It is," Max agreed. "But they wouldn't have found love if I hadn't helped them along."

"You call it help, I call it interference."

His father threw up his hands in frustration and startled his horse into dancing sideways. He patted the animal's neck and made a shushing sound. "Easy there."

"The thing is, Dad, you can check me off your conscience. It's all good. I don't need your help because I already did commit and I don't want to do it again. I lost the woman I love just when I thought I had everything. Wren turned us into a family but I lost Lara. Suddenly my perfect family was gone. So, committing cost me everything."

"That's the way I felt about your mother," Max said sadly. "But I was only thinking of myself when I kept her away from you boys. I thought she'd come around but instead I hurt my children. I'm really sorry, son."

"I believe you."

Oddly enough, Hunter understood. As a kid he'd been confused and hurt when his mom disappeared. Always in the back of his mind was the thought that maybe if he'd been a better kid she might not have gone away. If he'd never fallen in love with Lara, he wouldn't get it that a man could do stupid things because of love. He should be mad, but in a weird way he was bonding with his father, maybe for the first time.

"And it's okay, Dad."

"No, it's not. I started to realize it when Wren was born and Lara died. A man's perspective changes when he becomes a grandfather. I watched you hurting and raising her without a mother. That had me soul-searching. You didn't have a choice about losing your daughter's mother, but I did and chose wrong."

"Let me see if I understand this right.

You're blaming this recent matchmaking insanity of yours on my daughter?"

"No. Maybe." Max shrugged. "Lara's been gone six years, son. She wouldn't want her daughter growing up without a mother or you to be stuck in the past."

That struck a chord. When Lara's due date had been fast approaching, she'd started to get nervous about giving birth. But she'd taken it a step further and told him if anything happened to her she wanted him to fall in love and be happy again. It was as if she'd had a premonition that something was going to happen to her. But Hunter had blown her off. He'd told her childbirth was the most natural thing in the world and nothing would go wrong. But it had and losing her at what should have been the happiest time of their lives was the worst moment of his. He never wanted to feel like that again.

"Look—" He spotted a problem in the fencing and pointed. A post was tilting and nearly halfway to the ground, pulling the wire down on either side of it. "Need to prop that up."

Finally, something to do and get Max off his case.

They stopped and dismounted, dropping the reins to ground tie the horses. The well-trained animals would stand still and not run off while he and Max handled the repair. His dad held the post upright while Hunter dug the hole deeper with the small hand shovel he'd brought along with the other tools. Then he packed the dirt in tighter.

"There. That ought to do it. This will hold now. We caught it just in time." And the interruption had the added benefit of distraction.

"Looks good, son," his dad agreed.

They swung back into their saddles and continued the ride and fence inspection. Hunter was enjoying the sun, solitude and silence, until Max started in again, right where he'd left off.

"So, I got a call from Vivienne Dalton."

"Who?" Hunter knew exactly who she was

but there was no reason he had to make this easy on his dad.

"Come on, son. You know darn well she's the wedding planner working to find—"

"Women for your sons."

"You make it sound unsavory," Max accused. "I'm paying her to find suitable women for marriage. All you have to do is meet them. Believe it or not I'm doing this for your happiness."

"I'm already happy," Hunter insisted.

"Let me try this another way. My granddaughter needs a mother."

"She has Merry."

On the trip back from Avery and Finn's wedding, Hunter had received his daughter's message loud and clear. She was growing up and needed a female's guiding hand. He'd fixed the problem.

"I'm talking about a mother," Max emphasized. "Not someone who is paid to take care of her."

Right. Hunter signed her paycheck and Merry had taken the job because she needed the money. She was an employee. But he had a bad habit of forgetting that when he came in the door after a long workday and she greeted him with a heart-stopping smile and a hot meal on the table. Or when she spontaneously hugged Wren and kissed her cheek. That natural impulsive affection wasn't because of an hourly wage. It came from the heart.

He should probably thank his father for the reminder because forgetting he was her boss could be dangerous. The last thing he wanted was to fall in love again. Been there, done that. He was fine now and would pass on a repeat.

"Look, son, I've made questionable decisions in the past, but I'm trying to make up for it. Vivienne Dalton is a very nice woman and she isn't going to recommend someone unsuitable. And there's someone she would like you to meet."

"Okay."

Max looked at him funny. "Okay what?"

"I will think about meeting the woman Vivienne has vetted."

"Excellent. That's all I ask." His father beamed with approval.

He would agree to almost anything so they could talk about something else. But Hunter found himself wishing Merry was the woman the matchmaker had in mind. Which only proved he'd lost his.

Merry felt as if she'd been thrown into the deep end of the pool—the Crawford family pool, that is. On Thanksgiving. Sure, she'd attended the wedding with all of them, but she'd stayed in the background as Wren's nanny. It hadn't been quite two weeks since she'd started her full-time job for Hunter along with doing her darnedest to control this pesky attraction to him.

Now it was a traditional family holiday and all of them were gathered at the ranch's main house. Most of them were in the other room watching football while she was essentially hiding in the kitchen. It was big and functional although it could definitely use some renovation. But there was a huge sink and a big, if old-fashioned, island with lots of work space. She was helping to prepare dinner for thirteen. Fourteen if you counted little Sophia.

Lily Crawford was doing the cooking. She was a chef and recently married to Xander, third eldest of the brothers. She worked part time at Maverick Manor and not long ago started Lily's Home Cookin', preparing individual meals for customers. Word was spreading and she was steadily building her business.

Today Merry had volunteered to do the grunt work, slicing, dicing, cutting and chopping—anything that would make fixing this meal easier. She would have been nearly immobilized by the pressure of preparing a perfect holiday dinner but the other woman looked serene and confident, as if she was enjoying it. As if she was completely in her element. Which, of course, she was.

Merry was now peeling potatoes, letting

the skins fall on newspaper spread over the counter. There was a giant pot in front of her filled with water and she dropped the naked spuds into it. Lily was putting together snacks for the football crowd. She slid a cookie sheet of mini-quiches into the oven, then began to artfully arrange a cheese, raw vegetables and fruit platter.

"You are truly amazing," Merry said in awe.

"It's all about loving what I do. I suppose that's true of any profession. From what I saw at the wedding, you are pretty amazing with Wren." Lily looked up and smiled warmly. "She adores you."

"The feeling is mutual." *And I hope I'm good at it,* she thought. "But you're right. I do love kids."

"It shows." Lily arranged cucumber slices in a circle with berries in the center. "I can't thank you enough for your help. It saved me so much time."

"It's the least I could do. And a bonus for me that we've gotten better acquainted."

"Yes," she agreed. "That was a hectic weekend and I felt as if we were ships passing in the night."

"Plus, there are a lot of Crawfords." Merry put a peeled potato into the pot and picked up another one. "I wanted to put name tags on everyone to keep them straight."

"I can see how it might be confusing." Lily laughed. "But I have three older brothers so being around this family seems pretty natural to me."

"You're lucky to have siblings. No sisters?"

"No." She sighed. "But I wished for one."

"Me, too," Merry said.

"So you're an only child?"

"No." Although it felt that way to her. "I have a brother. Jack. He's ten years older."

"That's a big age difference. When you were five he was fifteen and in high school and might not have wanted a little sister tagging along. It must have been hard to be close."

"What makes you say that?"

"Your face." The other woman's expression

was sympathetic. "You've probably been told this before, but never play poker. Everything you feel is right there."

Yikes! Merry thought. She hoped that wasn't entirely true or she was going to have to work on that. This job with Hunter could get awkward otherwise, and she really needed it.

"It's more than age with Jack and me. There's actual geographical distance. When our mom died, he was eighteen and joined the military right out of high school. He's made it a career and has been gone a lot. I barely see him. He came to our dad's funeral but left right after." It had been nothing more than a duty to him. Being a career soldier taught him about that but nothing about family, or the fact that Merry had needed him to stay for just a little while.

"I'm sorry for your loss. I know it was recent," Lily said. "And it sounds like you didn't have a lot of support."

"From my friends here in Rust Creek Falls, but not family." The rejection still hurt. "It was hard being alone. And I think about that with Wren. I don't want that for her. A sibling would be—"

Merry stopped. She felt as if she'd known Lily far longer than she had and the woman was way too easy to talk to. That was her only excuse for bringing up something as personal as Hunter giving his daughter a brother or sister. That wasn't a topic the hired help should be discussing with his sister-in-law.

Heat crept into her cheeks as she met Lily's gaze. "Sorry. I think I said too much."

"Even if I agree with you?" Lily asked. "Did you see Wren with Sarah and Logan's baby? That child would be such a wonderful big sister."

"I know, right?"

"And, I may be spreading gossip, but this is Rust Creek Falls after all." The other woman smiled mischievously. "I think Avery's got a little baby bump going on."

Merry was busy with her job at school and Wren. Other than the wedding, she hadn't seen much of the newly married couple. "Really?"

"Yup. She's at that stage where a first thought might be that she's put on a couple pounds, but if you look closely, it's all tummy. In the cutest possible way. And the move to the hunting cabin. Fixing it up. If that's not nesting, I don't know what is."

"Wren will be so thrilled," Merry said. "She'd love to have a sister or brother, but a new cousin is the next best thing."

"Something sure smells good in here."

Merry didn't expect to hear a man's voice and this one belonged to Hunter. She dropped the potato she was holding and peeled a small chunk from her index finger. "Ouch."

"Are you okay?" Hunter quickly moved beside her and took her hand to assess the damage. "Doesn't look too bad."

"It's fine." Although the scrape stung like crazy. Even though she tried to pull away, he didn't let go and looked concerned. That was like chocolate and chips to her needy hormones. Suddenly she felt no pain and figured this attraction was good for something. "I'm just clumsy."

"I doubt that. Let's wash this off." He turned on the spigot beside them and gently held her wounded finger under the cold water to wash the blood away.

"Here's a bandage and some antibiotic cream." Lily set the things on the counter next to him. "These are staples in my kitchen, as important as the right ingredients. When you're using sharp instruments there are always accidents."

"Thanks," he said.

Merry was shaking but not from her mishap. It was a reaction to the nearness of this man and having him touch her. She'd done the same thing when they'd danced at the wedding. It seemed like forever since that night and her body was quivering with excitement. She really hoped he didn't notice.

He dried off her finger with a paper towel, dabbed on some ointment, then snugly wrapped the sticky adhesive strip around the wound. "It's tight to stop the bleeding. How does it feel?"

So good she didn't want him to stop touching her. But that's not what he meant. And when he continued to look at her, she hoped Lily was wrong about everything she felt being right there on her face.

"It's good," Merry finally said.

"Not too tight?"

"Nope. Everything is fine." She glanced at Lily, who was watching the exchange with great interest, until a timer sounded and she took the little quiches out of the oven. "So, I'm sure you didn't come in here to provide first aid."

Actually, Merry wouldn't have needed it if he hadn't come in here. Her arms and legs seemed to go limp and malfunction every time she saw him.

"What can we do for you, Hunter?" Lily asked. "I'm just putting the finishing touches on snack platters."

With his attention off her now, Merry's brain functioned normally again. "Wren hasn't eaten since breakfast and it's after lunch now. She must be starving."

"She hasn't said anything. Too busy playing princess with Genevieve."

"Our Genevieve?" Lily looked surprised. "The tomboy who does horse pedicures?"

"The same one." Hunter grinned but it quickly disappeared. "Knox said she's practicing for having kids."

"Wren would love more cousins," Merry commented but the look on his face made her want those words back.

"I was just saying how much Wren loves baby Sophia. I think she'd be excited about having more kids around." Lily's expression was innocent, but her green eyes glittered with mischief.

Hunter held up his hands to form a T, the signal for time-out. "I just came in for snacks, not a Crawford family population increase debate."

Merry was feeling a little sorry for him. He was looking cornered and uncomfortable. "And it's two against one."

"Okay. We'll let you off the hook." The other woman finished putting the little quiches on a tray. "I'll help you carry these into the family room."

"Great." He slid Merry a look that said "thank you" and took the fruit and cheese platter before making a speedy getaway.

Lily wasn't gone long and entered the room laughing. "Wow, that's a ravenous group in there. That food lost any artistic presentation almost before I put the tray down. And my Xander was leading the pack."

The woman's face turned loving and tender when she mentioned her husband. That made Merry curious.

"How did you and Xander meet?"

"Funny story." Lily smiled softly. "As everyone knows, Max is trying to get his sons to settle down and made a deal with Viv Dalton to set them up. I was supposed to go out with Knox—reluctantly, I should add. He canceled at the last minute."

"So you went out with Xander instead?"

"He came to apologize for his bonehead

brother and ended up taking me to dinner. I'm pretty sure he felt sorry for me because I'd been dumped. I'd even changed back into my jeans and T-shirt and was all ready to go."

"That was very sweet of him," Merry said.

"Yeah. He'd gotten my attention once before when I met all the guys at the same time. But he pretty much had me at that adorable gesture." She looked up. "Don't get me wrong. We had our ups and downs. Complications to maneuver. Compromises to make. But none of it was any match for love. We both fell hard." She sighed dreamily.

"So, you're happy?"

"Very."

"And I guess in a convoluted way Max was responsible for you two meeting," Merry commented. "But why would he feel he has to help his sons?"

"Apparently he had a rocky relationship with their mother and she abandoned the family when Wilder was a baby. It seems all the brothers have trouble committing. It's just a guess, but I think Max feels responsible somehow and is trying to help. To make it up to them."

Merry knew how it felt to lose her mom to illness but couldn't understand a woman voluntarily walking away from six children. That would surely leave a mark. Except... "But Hunter was married. Obviously he was able to get past the childhood trauma and take a chance."

"True. And his wife died." There was sympathy and sadness in Lily's expression.

"So he won't give it another try?"

"According to Xander he did eventually start to date again back in Texas, but his heart wasn't in it."

"Doesn't surprise me. From what I can see, he only has room in his heart for his daughter."

"I'm not so sure about that."

The teasing tone and mischievous twinkle in the other woman's eyes made Merry wonder. Did her face give something away when Hunter was in the kitchen? Good Lord, she hoped not. It was more likely that Max was trying to set up his son with someone appropriate, someone Viv Dalton had personally selected.

She didn't like the idea of that one bit, but no one asked for her opinion. She'd been hired to take care of Wren, not get involved with the child's father. Their business association took her out of the dating pool, which made her equal parts mad and sad.

And she had no right to either emotion.

Chapter Seven

Hunter was having the best first Thanksgiving in Rust Creek Falls. His family was together and even bigger now that four of his brothers were married. And then there was Merry. She was a breath of fresh air. Even her name was happy and she lived up to it every day. Case in point: when she took a chunk out of her finger peeling potatoes. She'd smiled through the first aid that had given him an excuse to get close to her. He wasn't proud of it, but that didn't stop him from remembering it.

Crawfords were milling around the big

dining room, figuring out where to sit. Max claimed the armchair at the head of the table. The perfectly browned turkey and carving knife were placed in front of him. Merry had taken Wren to supervise handwashing and the two of them returned to stand beside Hunter.

"Daddy, I want to sit in the chair next to Sophia's high chair."

Hunter looked at Logan and Sarah, who were close enough to hear.

"That sounds perfect," the baby's mother said. "And I'll sit on the other side."

Wren clapped her hands. "This is the best Thanksgiving ever!"

"Be sure to duck when she starts throwing her food instead of eating it," Logan teased. "And watch out when she puts cranberry sauce in her hair."

"Gross." Wren wrinkled her nose.

"Don't be so quick to judge." Hunter put his hand on her slight shoulder. "You did the same thing when you were her age."

"I don't believe you." His little girl put on her stubborn pouty face.

"That sounds so adorable," Merry said. "I wish I could have seen it. Do you have pictures?"

"Probably not."

There weren't many photos of his little girl's first year. Between ranch work and caring for an infant, he'd been pretty overwhelmed. His focus was on the day-to-day needs of their child. Memorializing that dark time with photos hadn't been high on his priority list.

"I'm going to move this along." Max took charge and told everyone where to sit.

"You're putting me at the foot?" Wilder asked.

"Consider it a metaphor. Maybe that will give you a kick in the—" Max winked at Wren "—backside and knock some sense into you."

The youngest Crawford took his place and grinned across the expanse of the big table at his father. "I'm perfectly happy with the amount of sense I have."

"Well, I'm not." Max watched everyone take the places he'd assigned.

Hunter pulled out Merry's chair and whispered, "My little brother doesn't have enough sense to know he has no sense."

"I heard that," Wilder said.

"Okay." Max picked up the carving utensils. "I'm going to cut this bird and we'll start passing the food around."

Everyone started to talk and the noise level rose. Hunter sneaked a look at Merry and thought she seemed a little tense and sad. Maybe she was intimidated by so many Crawfords in one place. Or maybe she felt out of place because she was his employee. He had a hard time remembering that because she seemed to fit so seamlessly into Wren's life. But this was also her first holiday without her dad, and her brother was also missing.

He wished there was a way to fix this as easily as he had patched up her finger earlier.

"How's your wound?" he asked.

"My what?"

"The finger."

She looked at him and her cheeks flushed. "I think I'll live. But it has to be said, I don't think I've ever peeled so many potatoes at one time."

"Feeding this family is kind of like cooking for an army." It was supposed to be a lighthearted comment to make her smile. It didn't. "Did I say something wrong?"

"What? No." She shook her head. "It just made me think about my brother for a second. I haven't spent a holiday with him since I was a little girl."

Hunter could have kicked himself for making her look so lost. Somehow he needed to snap her out of it because he wanted her to live up to her name again. And she was here to get through the first holiday without her dad.

He looked around the table at his brothers, remembering the testosterone-fueled squabbles they'd had over the years. There were a few black eyes and fat lips in all of their pasts. "We could have used a referee when I was growing up."

Her look was sympathetic, as if she knew their family scandal. "But now I bet you're glad to have every one of your brothers."

She was right. He loved them and wished each one a life filled with love and not loss like the one he'd experienced.

Finally Max, with pointers from Lily, had finished with the turkey and everyone started passing bowls and platters of food. When plates were full, their father announced that the annual what-I'm-thankful-for rounds would commence. Of course, as head of the family, he would start, then it would proceed from eldest to youngest.

"I'm thankful for all of my sons and their new brides. I'm grateful for this wonderful meal, prepared by all of you, especially our resident chef, Lily." She blushed as everyone applauded. Then he looked at Sophia and Wren with raw tenderness on his rugged face. "And I'm more grateful than I can say for these beautiful children, the next generation of Crawfords."

Everyone voiced their approval and there was some not very subtle sniffling from Avery. Wilder jumped in before his brothers could take their turns.

"I'd just like to say that I love all my new sisters-in-law, but, man, I'm glad to be single."

A chorus of boos drowned out the rest of his words but he only grinned. Hunter had mixed feelings.

The sound of a utensil tapping on a glass got his attention and he looked up. Finn was standing at the table, gazing down at Avery with an expression that revealed he was nuts about her.

"My wife and I have something special to be thankful for this Thanksgiving. We're going to have a baby." Spontaneous cheers, applause and hugs followed the reveal. "We wanted to keep the news just for us but we've known for a while."

"So have we," Logan and Sarah said together.

"Us, too," Genevieve said. "The glow. The baby bump."

"Am I showing?" Avery put a hand to her tummy.

"Just a little," everyone chimed in.

The mother-to-be sighed. "At least you didn't think I was just getting fat."

"You look beautiful," Finn assured her. "And I'm going to be a father."

"Better you than me, big brother," Wilder said. "I'm not a dirty diaper–changing kind of guy.

"So I'm gonna have another baby cousin?" Wren asked. When assured that she was right, she said, "Cool. I can't wait. This is the best holiday ever."

Hunter had to disagree. Except for Logan and their dad, he was the only other father in the room. The rest of them were gushing about wanting to expand their families, have babies. They couldn't wait. Even Wren couldn't wait.

Everyone was so happy and he couldn't say anything. All he had to offer was a warning about what could happen and he didn't want to bring everyone down. But it would terrify him if Merry was pregnant.

Whoa. Where the hell did that thought come from? Except he knew. He'd seen her bleed a little while ago and wanted to fix it. Because in spite of all his own warnings, he wasn't just starting to feel. He was starting to care. And that had to stop.

Hunter had been very quiet during dinner. Merry noticed because he'd been uncharacteristically chatty when they'd first sat down. She'd gotten the feeling he was trying to cheer her up. Go figure. Then Finn and Avery had made what should have been a happy announcement and his brothers and their wives had talked eagerly about starting families, too. Wilder had been outspoken in his aversion, but Hunter had clammed up.

They were home now and Merry was in the upstairs bathroom overseeing Wren's quick shower. The little girl was tired and needed to be in bed ASAP. When the water shut off, Merry was ready with a towel. After Wren dried off, she put on her favorite princess nightgown.

"I'll give your hair a quick brush, sweetie."

"Okay." The one word was followed by a big yawn. A few minutes later Wren climbed into her bed.

Merry pulled the covers up over her. "I'll go get your dad to read."

"But I want you to do it," the little girl said.

"Sweetie, your dad always reads to you. It's your thing." Merry felt a tingling at the base of her neck and somehow knew that Hunter was in the doorway hearing this. A moment later Wren confirmed her feeling.

"Daddy, I want Merry to read to me tonight and give me a good-night kiss."

He walked over to the bed and looked down at his daughter. There was no way you could miss the troubled expression on his face before he forced a smile. "Whatever you want, honey. Is it okay if I kiss you, too?"

"Yes, Daddy." She reached out her little arms and he bent down, then swallowed her slight frame in a big hug.

"I love you." His voice was gruff with emotion and some hurt feelings he was trying to hide. As always, he kissed her forehead. "See you in the morning."

"Love you," she said before yawning again.

Merry wanted to say something to Hunter but didn't know what. Even if she came up with the right words, it wasn't appropriate to discuss this in front of Wren. There was a slump to his broad shoulders when he left the room.

"I want the princess story," Wren said sleepily.

It was in a book of fairy tales, her favorite, and was on the nightstand beside the bed. Merry picked it up and started reading. "Once upon a time…"

A few paragraphs later she saw that the child was sound asleep. Merry set the book down and kissed the girl's sweet little cheek before tiptoeing out. Normally she would go to her bedroom and read, avoiding her employer and her crush on him. But not to-night. She needed to talk to him and make sure he understood that kids were change-able, temperamental and moody. Especially after a long, busy day.

She found him sitting on the sofa in the front room with a tumbler of liquor in his hand while staring at a blank TV screen. His back was to her.

"Hunter? Are you okay?"

He took a sip from his glass but didn't look in her direction. "I'm fine. Kids are unpre-dictable. Don't worry about it."

"Okay. Good. I wanted to make sure you were aware of that and didn't take offense to her asking for me. Because you are the most important person to her."

"I know." His voice was flat, empty of emotion, and then he drained the liquor in one swallow. When she didn't leave, he looked up and said, "Is there something else?"

"Yes." Stiffly, she sat on the end of the

sofa, carefully leaving enough room between them for at least two people. "You got very quiet tonight at dinner. Why?"

"I had nothing to add to the conversation."

"Oh, please. You were talking my ear off until your brother announced Avery was expecting. Then you looked as if someone cut the stirrups off your favorite saddle. Why?"

"You're my daughter's nanny. It's not information you need to do your job."

His tone wasn't angry, abrupt or condescending, which, oddly enough, concerned her more. This felt too controlled. "I disagree. Something's bothering you. Wren is going to notice. Maybe instinctively she already did and that's why she asked me to step in for the bedtime story. I need something so I know how to respond when she asks why her daddy got quiet and stopped smiling."

He set his empty glass on the table beside him and seemed as if he was going to walk away without a word. But then he released a long sigh and looked at her. "Her mother died."

"I know. When she was a baby." But Merry was extremely curious about what happened. She wasn't proud of that but she was only human. "But I don't understand—"

"It's my fault."

"What?" She couldn't believe she'd heard right.

Dark intensity glittered in his eyes. "Wren was a couple days old and Lara complained of headaches, blurred vision and upper abdominal pain. I found out later all are classic symptoms of eclampsia. A complication of pregnancy."

She was quiet for a moment, then hesitantly asked, "But what is it?"

"High blood pressure that caused seizures and compromised her kidneys and other organs. Mostly it's diagnosed during prenatal visits and treated. It's rare to show up after birth but we drew the short straw on that." Bitterness squeezed every single word.

"That's so awful I don't even know what to

say." Merry didn't want to look at the misery on his face but couldn't seem to look anywhere else. "But I also don't understand why you blame yourself."

He dragged his fingers through his hair. "I fell for her and wanted to marry her when I was a college senior and she was a freshman. But I didn't want to marry too young like my dad, didn't want to make the same mistakes he did."

In the interest of full disclosure she said, "Lily told me that your mother abandoned her children when you were all really young."

"I was about Wren's age. More than once I thought that if I'd been a better kid she wouldn't have left." He shrugged. "So Lara and I waited and got married right out of college. Both of us wanted kids, but she got a job with a Dallas TV station and was working hard, hoping to be promoted to on-air anchor."

"But?" There had to be one.

"After a year I wanted to start the family we'd talked about. She finally gave in because she wanted me to be happy." He looked anything but. "A classic example of be careful what you wish for."

She didn't know what to say and asked, "What's the second reason?"

"Wren was two days old when Lara's symptoms started. I wanted to take her to the emergency room but she insisted it would pass. She refused to leave her baby—" He stopped for a moment and pressed his lips together. "I should have insisted. Should have picked her up bodily and made her go."

"You're not a doctor, Hunter. You couldn't know what would happen."

"No. But if I'd been a better husband she would still be alive."

So, there was still some of that little boy in him, the one who felt if he'd been better his mother wouldn't have left. Merry sighed. "So you were remembering all of this when Avery revealed that she was pregnant."

He nodded, and when he looked at her, the worry was more focused. "Everyone forgets about the bad things that can happen, but I lived it. At dinner all they talked about was the warm, fuzzy part of having babies. Everyone was over the moon. But I just can't get excited. Something—" he touched his chest "—something is stopping me."

"Oh, Hunter." She couldn't stand to be so far away from him and crossed the distance between them until she could feel the heat from his body. She touched his arm. "I understand why you feel this way. But you said the condition is rare. You couldn't know what was going to happen. Hindsight is twenty-twenty and if you could do it differently, surely you would."

He nodded but said nothing.

"Someday you're going to have to tell Wren. So she knows her family medical history."

There was a tortured expression in his eyes when he met her gaze. "Oh, God—"

She knew exactly where his mind went. That the same fate awaited Wren one day. "Don't go there. But this is the reason doctors want medical history." She waited until the fear on his face receded. "But if you tell her it's your fault her mother died, that would be a lie. And you don't strike me as the kind of man who doesn't tell the truth. To Wren or anyone else."

"I try to stick to the facts."

"And the fact is, Wren's mother made a choice. You honored her wishes."

He thought about that for a few moments, then nodded and almost smiled. "How did you get so good at making someone feel better?"

"I'm no stranger to having a loved one taken away."

"Gosh, Merry, I'm sorry." He put his hand over hers where she'd left it on his arm. "This is the first holiday without your dad and I made it all about me."

"It's understandable."

"No. I'm an idiot. Tell me about your dad."

"Are you sure?" she asked.

"Yes."

His spirit seemed lighter after talking about his feelings. Maybe it would work for her. "When Mom died and my brother left home, Dad didn't quite know what to do with me when he was working. There were after-school programs or a neighbor lady sometimes watched me. But when he couldn't find somewhere to leave me, he took me with him on his electrical jobs." She smiled. "People called him Sparky. And I learned a lot about sockets, wires and circuit breakers."

"I'll keep that in mind." Hunter smiled.

Merry was glad she was already sitting down. The grin transformed his face and he was so handsome her knees went weak. She cleared her throat and continued. "Dad was good at what he did and was busy most of the time, but on a rare day when he was home, we hunkered down and hung out together."

"Doing what?"

"Chores. Playing games. But our favorite thing was watching old movies. He always said they don't make 'em like that anymore."

"We can do that now." He half turned to

grab the remote control from the table beside him.

Merry's hand slid off his arm. She was both horrified that touching him felt so darn natural and wistful that the contact was over. Then her head cleared and she realized what he was doing.

"That's okay. I don't want to bore you with old movies," she said.

"Hey, who says it will bore me?" He challenged her with a look. "Besides, you cheered me up. I'm returning the favor. Call it a tribute to your dad."

With the remote he turned on the flat screen TV, then pulled up the guide and scrolled through until finding the channel he wanted. Hunter leaned back and relaxed into the sofa. He held up a fist and said, "Here's to Sparky."

Merry bumped his fist with hers and the TV screen blurred as tears gathered in her eyes. She settled in next to Hunter and said, "Dad would have loved this."

She loosened up and the heat from Hunter's body warmed her, made her drowsy after a while. Her eyes drifted closed and she dozed off. She woke with her head on Hunter's shoulder, not sure how long she'd been out. But the movie credits were scrolling by so it had been a while.

Hunter's breathing was soft, even, and she knew the tryptophan had claimed another victim. She was reluctant to move and wake him. Mostly she was reluctant to move and end the closeness of their bodies.

While she hesitated, the decision was taken out of her hands because he was looking at her.

"Hi," he said, smiling drowsily. His gaze was unguarded and open, revealing raw, unconcealed need.

He slowly lowered his head, tilting it the way a man did to kiss a woman. Merry's heart started to hammer and she could hardly breathe. Anticipation and excitement hummed through her as her eyelids drifted closed.

Then she felt him freeze and her eyes

popped open. The happy, sleepy smile was gone, replaced by a bitter twist of his lips.

"I'm sorry, Merry."

In her head she was telling him not to be, but the words stayed where they were.

"That was inappropriate," he said. "It's wrong to put you in this position."

Not if she wanted to be there. "Hunter—"

"Good night." He stood and went upstairs.

Merry tried not to be crushed but wasn't very successful. And knowing how he'd lost his wife and why he was so protective of his daughter didn't help much. It made clear only that he was determined to keep her firmly in her nanny role and at a distance. Unfortunately, the "almost" kiss made it clear how much she wanted him. He also made it clear that she was never going to have him.

Chapter Eight

Hunter couldn't believe himself.

He'd come within a whisper of kissing Merry and that was why he was sitting in a booth at Ace in the Hole with a woman Vivienne Dalton had vetted for him. The whole thing came under the heading of "it seemed like a good idea at the time."

So, he'd said something to Max, who put Viv on the case and she'd set up a meet for the Saturday after Thanksgiving. He'd met Everly Swanson, an attractive brown-eyed brunette, at the local low-key establishment. There was a scarred bar on the far wall and booths around the perimeter. A wooden dance floor with scattered tables was in the center. In the window, a large neon sign of an ace of hearts blinked off and on, along with one that advertised beer.

Everly seemed like a perfectly nice woman, but now he had to make conversation.

She beat him to it. "So, tell me about yourself."

"Okay." He thought about where to start. "I went to Texas A&M, where I was a farm and ranching major. I'm originally from Texas and it's my humble opinion that ranching is the best job in the world—" He was relieved when the bar's owner arrived and stood at the end of their booth.

"Hey, Rosey," Everly said.

"Hey there, lady. It's nice to see you." She gave him a curious look. "Hunter Crawford. Been a while. It's nice to see you. With Everly. Is there romance in the air?"

"I think that's burgers and fries you're smelling," he said.

"Could be."

Rosey Traven was a curvaceous woman in her sixties. Hunter knew she made it her business to find out what was going on in the personal lives of her customers. He'd come into the Ace a couple of times with Wilder, who kept pushing him into being a wingman. Hunter did his best but it never went well.

Kind of how he expected this evening to go.

"What can I get you?" Rosey looked at each of them.

"Are you ready to order?" he asked the woman across from him.

"I am. I'll have the usual, Rosey."

"Burger basket, no cheese and a glass of red wine. Got it." The older woman looked at him. "For you?"

"Burger basket, with cheese. And a beer."

"Coming right up. I'll get those drinks out in a jiffy." She smiled at them then sashayed away.

"She's sure a character," Everly said. "Don't

you love those jeans, boots and that belted peasant top?"

"You mean all women of a certain age don't dress like that?"

"Like a pirate queen? No." She laughed. "But don't let the outfit fool you. That woman has a soft heart and a knack for giving love a helping hand if she thinks two people are made for each other."

"Okay." He tried not to squirm on the faux leather bench seat.

"Since you're pretty new to town you probably don't know Rosey's story." When he shook his head, she elaborated. "She and her husband, Sam, own Ace in the Hole. He's the former navy SEAL who worked to win her heart and become the love of her life. She'd probably never admit it, but she wants everyone to be as happy as she and Sam are."

Well, damn. This "date" was the opposite of romance. The point was to get his father off his back and Merry out of his system, not do the romance dance. Color him a bonehead for not going somewhere less public and prone to gossip. He intended to get through it by walking a fine line—friendly, but not too friendly. He didn't want to give this woman, or anyone else, ideas.

"Tell me about you." He hoped to get her talking about herself, a safer subject than his life.

"I do clerical work in the mayor's office. I actually grew up here in Rust Creek Falls, but lived over in Bozeman when I was married…but I'm not now." Her lips pressed tightly together for a moment, then she relaxed. "Is there anyone special in your life?"

Merry. The thought was suddenly there. She was special because she took great care of his daughter. At least that's what he told himself. Her qualities appealed to him, and not just the ones that had his little girl behaving like an angel. Merry was sexy and made him laugh. It was a dynamite combination. And none of that was what Everly meant. "I have a daughter. Wren. She's six."

"Adorable name." Her smooth forehead puckered a little. "I confess that Viv Dalton told me your wife passed away after your daughter was born. That must have been hard."

"Yes—"

A waitress walked over with a tray. "Here are your drinks, guys. Food is coming up shortly. Let me know if you need refills."

"Thanks," he said, then looked at the woman across from him and held up his longneck bottle of beer. "To new friends."

"Friends. Right." She lifted her glass and sipped. "So, you've been a single dad? How do you make that work?"

"I've had help from family and friends. My job is on the family ranch, which means that some chores can be scheduled around my daughter's needs. If they can't be, I used to call on one of my brothers or my dad."

"But you don't anymore?"

"No." He drank from his beer then set it on the cocktail napkin in front of him.

"Obviously she's school age, but she still needs supervision in the afternoons and summers. No?"

"Yes." He toyed with the bottle, reluctant to say more.

Everly wasn't letting him off the hook. "Why don't you call on your family for child care anymore?"

"It's not so easy now. Four of my brothers are married."

"So I heard." One of her eyebrows arched.

"Of course you did. This is a small town, not like Dallas."

She laughed. "So I don't have to explain how everyone knows your business."

"No." And that's why he should have taken her somewhere no one knew them. "But their priorities have shifted. Now my dad and brother Wilder are the only ones who could help me out. Little brother's judgment isn't up to my standards where my daughter is concerned. And my father is busy."

"So what are you going to do?"

"Already done. I hired Meredith Matthews to be her nanny."

"I've met Merry. She's beautiful—which I

could seriously dislike if she wasn't so darn nice."

The waitress showed up just then with their baskets and her timing couldn't have been better. They weren't supposed to be talking about him. How did that happen?

"There's ketchup on the table. Can I get you anything else?" the server asked. When they shook their heads, she said, "Enjoy and if you need anything, let me know."

Hunter dug into his burger as if he hadn't eaten in a month. You weren't supposed to talk with your mouth full, right? But way too soon his basket was empty.

Everly had more than half a burger left. She nibbled at her fries a bit, then said, "So, don't take this the wrong way, but this feels like a kind of forced date, rather than one you were dying to go on."

What was it with women? They could effortlessly carry on a conversation while chowing down on a messy hamburger and still look delicate and ladylike.

"I have to admit I'm here to get my father off my back. What gave me away?"

"You keep looking at the door." She didn't seem upset.

"I'm a little out of practice. Okay," he said, grinning slightly, "more than a little. Is that your way of giving me the brush-off?"

She grinned back. "If that was my plan, I'd have a friend call with a fake emergency. Or, better yet, I'd go to the ladies' room, then sneak out without a goodbye."

"But this *is* a brush-off." He wasn't an idiot, after all.

She shrugged. "I prefer to be direct. I think we both know there's no spark here. But it was nice to go out with a decent guy." She smiled—a little wistfully, he thought.

"You're right. And I appreciate your honesty." She *was* a nice woman—funny, smart, pretty. It wasn't her fault that she didn't have striking hazel eyes and thick, curly blond hair. She couldn't help that she wasn't Merry. "I'm sorry."

"Don't apologize. I would rather know the

truth. And a dinner is always appreciated. As is meeting new friends."

"I'd like to be friends," he said.

"Me, too." She took the paper napkin off her lap and wadded it up to toss in her half-empty basket. "But would you mind a word of advice?"

"Probably."

"Too bad. You're getting it anyway." She laughed, then turned serious. "You've been hurt in the worst way possible. I can see why you think it's important to control your feelings and protect yourself. But take it from me, that's impossible. Feelings and emotions have a mind of their own. They have a way of sneaking up on you when you least expect it. And that's not a bad thing."

"Sounds like you've had experience. From your divorce, I guess?"

"Yeah. But I won't bore you with the details." She gave him a smile before sliding out of the booth. "Thanks for dinner, Hunter. Really. And remember, feelings can't be controlled."

Hunter watched her walk to the old screen door. There was a loud squeak when she opened it and let herself out.

He knew she was right about not being able to control his feelings, and he didn't like it. If he could, he wouldn't have been counting the minutes until he could politely leave and go home. And this feeling wasn't new. It got stronger every day when he found reasons to put off a chore so he could get back to the cabin and see Merry.

That made it official. He was in hot water. His child care issue was solved but the solution had created an even bigger problem.

"Daddy went out with a lady."

"Yes, he went to meet someone," Merry agreed.

They were sitting at the kitchen table eating grilled cheese sandwiches and chicken noodle soup. It was the little girl's favorite and Merry decided it might be good for the soul. She was wrong. After one bowl her soul was still not happy about Hunter meeting a lady. And although it didn't matter how many times she reminded herself that his social life was none of her business, she couldn't reconcile the fact that he'd nearly kissed her and two days later he was hooking up with some floozy.

Well, that wasn't fair but she didn't think there was enough chicken soup on the planet to change her attitude. Still, she couldn't let Wren know how she felt.

"Sweetie, now that I'm here to take care of you, it's natural that your dad would want to go out with a woman."

"Why does he have to, Merry? He's got me."

This conversation could easily go in an awkward direction if she didn't choose her words carefully. The last thing she wanted was to tell Hunter she'd been forced to explain sex to his six-year-old daughter. She just couldn't say that the man probably went out because he wanted to sleep with her.

Merry had been ready to go there with him on Thanksgiving but he'd put the brakes on that. Since then she'd tried to convince herself he'd been right, but she wasn't quite buying that.

"Believe me, sweetie, there's nothing he loves more than spending time with you. But there are grown-up activities he wants to do." Darn it. That was going to generate follow-up questions. "Like going out to dinner. Or a movie."

"I like movies." Wren's little face was puckered in an adorable pout.

"Sometimes he might like one that's not about princesses or animated animals. There are a lot that he can't take you to see."

"But he doesn't have to take a lady. Uncle Wilder would go."

"Probably." And the handsome devil would hit on every single woman in the theater, dragging Hunter along with him. "Your uncle wants different things than your dad."

"This is all Gramps's fault." The little girl slurped some soup and sucked up a noodle while broth dribbled down her chin.

"Napkin, sweetie." Merry should have ignored that important and revealing information, but just couldn't. "What did your Gramps do?"

"He's paying that lady to get women to go out with my dad. I heard them talking. They didn't know I was there." She bit off the corner of her diagonally cut sandwich. "I like triangles."

"I'm glad. And we need to have a talk about listening to a conversation when the people talking don't know you're there."

Wren finished chewing her sandwich, then said, "But I wanted to hear what they were sayin'. They would've stopped if they knew I was there."

"Still, next time you should let them know you're there." Do as I say, not as I do, Merry thought, remembering the night she'd overheard father and daughter talking.

"Okay."

"So, did Gramps say why he wants your dad to meet women?"

"He said my mommy would want Daddy

to be happy. Gramps tells him that all the time."

"Well, Gramps knew your mom," Merry said gently. "So it's probably true."

"But I don't know the lady Daddy is with." There was a stubborn expression on her face and an angry look in her eyes. "And I'm mad at him. Aren't you mad at him?"

Merry could be on board with that, but she had no right to the feelings. Her responsibility was taking care of Wren, not having an opinion on her father's love life. Being conflicted made this a fine line to walk.

Best to sidestep the question entirely. "Well, sweetie, it might be a good idea for you to talk to your dad about this. Because he might go out with her again. If he likes her."

Just saying those words made Merry's chest feel tight and her soul didn't much care for it either.

"I don't like her already." She folded her arms over her thin chest. Talk about closed body language.

Merry was conflicted again, torn between gratitude that Wren approved of her and a duty to point out that she should give people a chance. She decided that conversation could wait until she was less emotionally at odds with herself. Less talk, more action to turn this evening around.

"Are you finished with dinner?" Merry asked.

The little girl put down her mostly eaten triangle and said, "I'm full."

"Okay. Do you want to make cookies?"

Wren's little face lit up and hostility disappeared. "The kind we can decorate?"

"Yes. With icing and sprinkles and red and green sparkles."

"Oh, boy!" She wiped her mouth then slid off her chair. "I'll take my dishes to the sink."

"Good girl. We'll wash these up real quick and make room for baking."

The child insisted on helping so "real quick" took a few minutes longer. Then Merry got out all the ingredients for her mother's sugar cookie recipe. She'd baked them with her mother as a child, and after her mom's passing, when she was old enough, she'd made them for her dad. They'd always shared memories of the woman both of them loved and missed. This year there was no one to remember with her and she was grateful to have Wren, the blessing of a child to take the sting out of this painful transition to her new holiday normal.

Together they measured everything into a big bowl and Merry let the little girl try mixing. Of course, the powdered ingredients floated over the side and her six-year-old attention span didn't last long. So Merry took over just as her mom had always done with her. Before long, the dough was ready to roll out and the oven was preheated with cookie sheets standing by to be filled.

Wren knelt on a kitchen chair in front of the flour-dusted breadboard with a small mound of dough in the center. "Can I roll it out?"

"Yes." Merry watched the child use the

rolling pin that had been her mother's and her vision wavered with unshed tears. Then Wren looked up at her and smiled happily, making her smile, too. It made her heart happy that time spent with her own mom could be channeled to bring joy to this motherless little girl.

Rolling went better than mixing, and Merry let her pick the holiday cookie cutters—a tree, star, Santa Claus, snowman, reindeer, wreath. The first pan was ready to go in the oven when the back door opened and Hunter walked in.

"Hi."

Merry blinked at him. "I didn't expect you home so early." Darn, what was it about this man that had her blurting out things she wouldn't ordinarily say?

"Yeah, well…" He didn't quite meet her gaze but gave his daughter a hug. "Hey, you."

"Daddy your face is cold." She giggled when he grabbed her in a bear hug and squealed when he put a cold hand on her neck. "Did you meet the lady?"

"Her name is Everly Swanson. And yes, I met her."

Merry knew the woman. Beautiful, smart, funny, charming. She was pretty much everything a man could want. She truly liked the woman but right this minute she was struggling with that.

Was she nice?" Wren demanded.

"She was." Hunter touched her cheek with his finger. "You've got flour all over your face."

"I know. Me and Merry are bakin'." She lasered him with a look. "Is she pretty?" |

"Yes."

A man would have to be crazy not to be attracted to the woman. Merry desperately wanted to take over the interrogation and find out, but that would be inappropriate. She pressed her lips together before more words escaped that would embarrass her.

"Did you go to the movies?" Wren asked him.

"No," he answered. "Why?"

"Merry said you wanted to meet ladies so you could take them to movies I can't see."

"We just had dinner at Ace in the Hole."

Not especially romantic, Merry thought. Although there were booths in dark corners. If sparks flew, you didn't need amped-up atmosphere. You could be sitting on the sofa in front of the TV and fall asleep with your head on his shoulder and—

"Are you gonna take her to the movies?" The hostility returned to that small face with a vengeance. "A movie that's not a cartoon?"

"I don't think so." He took off his sheepskin-lined jacket and hung it on a hook by the door.

Before he turned away, Merry thought he glanced at her and wondered what the funny look on his face was all about.

"Why don't you think you're gonna take her to the movies?" Apparently, Wren wouldn't be put off.

He walked back to the table where the little girl was still kneeling on the chair. Instead of answering, he studied the baking paraphernalia. "I'm pretty sure I don't have a rolling pin."

"That's mine. Or rather my mom's." Merry thought he didn't look much like a man who'd had a sparks-flying kind of dinner with a woman. He looked more like a man who would bring up ownership of a rolling pin to get out of talking about his evening. "I figured Wren and I would do some baking so I packed up some things and brought them over. Is that a problem?"

"No. I just wondered where it came from." He looked at her then. "Any action on the house?"

"I got an offer about a week ago and accepted it. Guess I forgot to tell you. And the couple want a short escrow so they can be in by Christmas."

"Is it a good offer?"

"Full price. My agent says the terms are good and fair." The loan would be paid off with not much left over after escrow costs. But as long as she was working for Hunter, she would have a roof over her head. Now she needed this job more than ever.

"Daddy?"

"Yeah, kiddo?"

"Did you kiss the lady?"

His brief reprieve was over and he looked acutely uncomfortable again. "I'm not sure that's something you need to know about."

"I think it is." Wren stood up on the chair but he was still taller. "Cuz if you did kiss her, we need to talk. And I need to meet her."

"Oh?" He glanced at Merry then back to his daughter. "And why is that?

"Because Merry said if you like her I have to talk about my feelings. And if you go out with her again, I should give her a chance before I decide I don't like her."

Hunter looked as if he wanted to both laugh and run for the hills. The courageous man stood his ground. "Okay, then. We don't have to talk because I didn't kiss her."

Wren's gaze narrowed and she put her hands on her hips. "Did she kiss you? Girls do that sometimes, kiss boys first."

"I don't want to know how you know that. And no. There was zero kissing. We had burgers and she left."

Merry hoped the huge grin she was rocking on the inside didn't show on the outside. She was unreasonably pleased that there was no chemistry with the woman. At least that was her guess. If there had been he wouldn't be home so early. And thanks to Wren, she knew no one had been kissed. She wanted to do a triumphant arm pump, then it occurred to her how self-centered she was being.

During the season of hope and giving, she was celebrating that her boss hadn't connected with someone. She couldn't have him but didn't want anyone else to have him either. What a horrible person she was.

A horrible person with a crush on her boss that didn't show any signs of going away. Her house was sold and she needed a place to live and extra income. This job was perfect and she couldn't do anything to mess it up.

Hello, rock and a hard place, she thought. Might as well introduce herself because she was stuck firmly between them.

Chapter Nine

Following church services the next day Hunter drove back to the ranch with Wren and Merry. This felt a lot like a family and when he'd walked in the door last night after being at Ace in the Hole with a woman, he'd felt a lot like a cheater. His daughter's questions didn't pull any punches either. *Did you kiss her?*

Heck, he'd never once even wanted to kiss her. But he had to give the woman credit. She was the one who'd told him it wouldn't work. And she didn't know the half of it.

He turned onto the road leading to the Ambling A, then glanced into the rearview mirror at his little girl secured in her car seat. "I have some work to do in the barn, kiddo. What do you and Merry have planned for this afternoon?"

"I want to go to the barn with you."

Words that he heard way too often and made his blood run cold. "Honey, we've talked about this—"

"But, Daddy, I want to see the barn cats and the goats and the horses," she pleaded. "Merry, tell him it's okay."

"Is there a problem?" the nanny asked.

He glanced at her in the passenger seat beside him, so pretty in a royal blue knit dress and knee-high black boots. Wren was looking to get the nanny on her side. But he'd bet she wouldn't bite the hand that signed her paycheck, or something like that.

"The barn can be a dangerous place for a curious little girl," he said.

"I'm not curious," Wren piped up.

Merry smothered a laugh. "*Curious* is her middle name."

"Tell me about it."

"But how is the barn unsafe?" she asked.

"Ranch tools. Pitchfork comes to mind. Also leather tools for tack and saddles' care and repair—knives, cutters, scissors and splitters."

"I won't touch anything," Wren promised. "Except the cats and goats."

"What about the horses?" he asked. To Merry he said in a voice meant for her ears only, "She's so little. The animals are big enough to crush her like a grape."

"I'm not that little." Wren had really good hearing. "And Merry is here. She can watch me if I get curious."

"She has a point." Merry shrugged. "Not taking sides here, but I could channel her natural curiosity in a safe way."

"Please, Daddy."

"It is what you're paying me for," Merry reminded him.

True enough. But he'd forgotten all about the boss/employee dynamic that night they'd fallen asleep watching a movie. He'd wanted so much to kiss her then and now still felt the ache of not doing it.

He glanced in the mirror again and the drama princess had her hands together in a prayerful, pleading way. Spineless, that's what he was where this child was concerned. "I guess that would be all right."

"Thank you, Daddy."

When they got to the cabin, everyone changed out of their church clothes. After a quick lunch, of which Wren ate very little in her excitement, the three of them walked to the barn. His brother Knox was there helping his wife, Genevieve, trim a horse's hooves and shoe them.

"Aunt Gen—" Wren started to run over to the woman but Merry put a hand on her shoulder.

"Careful, sweetie, you don't want to startle the horse."

"Hi, pumpkin. Merry's right. Give me a second."

Genevieve Crawford wasn't much over five feet tall and her wavy blond hair fell to the middle of her back. But she confidently hammered nails into the U-shaped metal shoe on the horse's hoof, then let the leg down into the hay. The woman straightened, then removed her gloves and tucked them into the back pocket of her worn jeans. She moved away from the animal to stand by the stall's open gate.

"Can I hug her now?" Wren asked the nanny.

"Yes." Merry removed her hand.

"Hi, Aunt Genevieve." The little girl threw herself into the other woman's arms. "When I grow up I want to give horses new shoes like you do."

Knox stood beside his wife and tugged playfully on the child's pigtail. "How does your dad feel about that?"

"He doesn't like me to come to the barn at all cuz there's sharp stuff. And he's afraid a horse will step on me."

"You saw the way she was rushing in just now," Hunter said in his defense. "If Merry hadn't stopped her—"

"She's six and that was normal," the nanny assured him. "But if she was here more often and learned appropriate behavior around the animals, that would minimize any risk."

Genevieve looked at her husband and they both nodded. "Merry's right."

Merry's expression was earnest. "She's a ranch kid. She lives here and there are animals. Teach her about them. Has she ever been on a horse?"

"No." Wren shot her dad a hostile look. "He won't let me. I keep asking and he keeps saying no."

The three adults stared at him as if he'd just lit his hair on fire. "It's my job to keep her safe. If anything happened to her—"

Merry put her hand on his arm. "You know better than anyone that life doesn't come with a guarantee. But it also needs to be lived. If you keep Wren from participating, she might be safe, but how happy will she be? What if Max had kept you and your brothers out of the barn and away from the horses?"

"Ouch." Knox made a nervous face. "That's a scary thought."

It was, Hunter admitted, if only to himself. "What if she gets hurt?"

"Teach her," Merry said again. "Make her barn safe and animal smart. Show her the right way to do things. Put her on a horse."

"Please, Daddy?" Wren clasped her hands together and gave him puppy dog eyes.

He hated puppy dog eyes because it worked every time. Along with Merry's common sense advice. Not to mention Knox and Genevieve giving him pitying looks. He was badly outnumbered. "Okay. But, Wren, you have to listen and do as I say."

"I promise, Daddy. Can you show me now?"

He wanted to say no but didn't think he could hold out against the peer pressure. Or maybe it was the reassuring touch of Merry's hand that made the decision feel right. And the encouragement and approval in her pretty hazel eyes. "I guess repairing the tack can wait."

"Yay!" Wren wrapped her arms around his waist in a spontaneous hug. "Thank you, Daddy."

"I know just the horse for her," Gen said to Knox.

He nodded. "That little pony. Charlotte."

Hunter knew which one his brother meant. A sweet, gentle, even-tempered animal. "I agree. Let's get her saddled. I'll show you how, kiddo."

"I'll help," Merry said.

Hunter led them to Charlotte's stall, then showed Wren the pad that went under the saddle.

"Pull it forward over her withers," Merry instructed, "then back where you'll be sitting. That will make sure the horse's hair is flat underneath the pad."

"Then lift the saddle onto the horse." Hunter did that.

"Place it gently like your dad did," Merry said. "You're not big enough yet to do this but when you are, don't slam it down. That could surprise Charlotte and spook her."

"Okay." Wren's eyes were big as saucers in her little face.

Hunter showed her how to take the cinch at one end and pull it through the buckle.

"Do it in stages," Merry added. "Loosely at first, to see what's right for Charlotte. You want the saddle secure but any tighter than that is an unnecessary discomfort for the horse."

Hunter showed her how to hold her hand out, palm up, so the horse could get her scent and become acquainted but not leave her fingers vulnerable. Then he demonstrated how to take the reins and walk slowly outside into the corral. Lifting the little girl, he coached her to put one pink-sneakered foot into the stirrup and swing her other leg over. And not to sit down too hard and startle the animal.

"Look at you on a horse." Merry smiled up at the little girl. "Way to go."

A huge grin lit up her face. "I want to ride now, Daddy."

"Let your dad show you how to hold the reins first, sweetie. And how to use them to make her stop, go and turn from side to side."

Hunter was impressed. There was more to Merry Matthews than just working in the classroom. She had some experience with horses and riding. Her knowledge showed again when she diplomatically reminded him not to overwhelm Wren with advanced techniques or too much information. He agreed and let her slowly walk the horse around the corral with him on one side and Merry on the other.

"You're doing great," he told her.

The little girl leaned forward and gently patted the horse's neck. "Good job, Charlotte."

After a few minutes he began to relax. He looked across the horse's rump and met Merry's gaze. "Is it just me, or is she a natural?"

"Not just you."

"I appreciate your help. It's hard not to keep giving her pointers."

"There's a readiness component to learning," she said. "You have to be comfortable with basics before moving to the next level."

He nodded. That made sense. And it occurred to him that his daughter might have gotten her curiosity gene from him. He couldn't resist saying, "And you've been holding out."

She looked surprised. "Oh?"

"I know you're good with kids and your dad was an electrician. But you know a lot about horses. How did you learn?"

"Oh. That." Suddenly Merry didn't look so merry.

"What?"

"My boyfriend works at one of the local ranches. He showed me some stuff."

Hunter didn't like the idea of her with another man, but that was none of his business. The only thing that should concern him was keeping her a happy employee who would stay on as the nanny and take good care of his daughter.

"You never mentioned a boyfriend. I'd have made sure you had time off to see him.

Just let me know if you have plans." The words nearly choked him and the idea of her with a guy showing her "stuff" about horses or anything else made him want to put his fist through a wall. It was hard to file this intense emotional response under employer responsibility.

"I don't need time." Her mouth twisted with disapproval. "I should have said *ex-*boyfriend. I broke up with him. When caring for my dad took up more and more of my time, the jerk flat out said if he didn't come first he was gone."

"So you beat him to it." He nodded. "Sounds like a good move."

"Yeah. My dad never liked him." She smiled a little sadly. "He had an opinion on every boy I've liked since I started liking boys in the fifth grade. And he was always right."

"I don't want to even think about Wren liking boys. Ever."

"Ew," came the little girl's voice from above them. "Boys are weird. And gross."

"They won't always be, sweetie." Merry grinned at him, then studied the child, who was starting to squirm in the saddle. "Is your tush getting tired yet, Wren?"

"A little."

Hunter took the hint. "You need to go easy the first time on horseback. Should we stop for today?"

"Good idea, Dad. Charlotte might be getting hungry."

"She might not have eaten very much lunch," Merry interjected.

"Yeah. We'll go in now. This probably isn't a good time to show you how to take care of Charlotte after you ride her."

"Can you show me next time?" Wren asked eagerly.

"Sure." He walked them back into the barn and tied the reins inside Charlotte's stall. He lifted Wren down and she hugged him tight.

"Thank you, Daddy. I can't wait to ride again."

"Okay."

That made him feel pretty great, but Merry

looked at him as if he'd hung the moon. And he wanted her to look at him like that again. He watched the little girl put her hand into the nanny's and chatter happily as they left the barn.

"Well, well, well…" Knox rested his arms on top of the stall fence. Genevieve was beside him looking like a cat who just caught a bird and dropped it at his feet.

"What?" he demanded.

"There's a spark between you and the nanny." His brother was grinning.

"Genevieve," he said, looking at his sister-in-law and doing his best to work up a teasing tone, "did you let your husband get kicked in the head by a horse?"

"No," she answered. "But even if he did have a head injury, he's not wrong. I saw it, too."

"Then both of you need your eyes examined. And maybe your heads, too. There's nothing between Merry and me except what's best for Wren."

"You do realize that when you bury your

head in the sand, you leave your ass exposed, right?" Knox pulled his wife close and kissed her lightly on the lips. "Trust me, I know all about these things."

Knox and Genevieve were seeing romantic sparks where none existed. They were dead wrong.

"But, Daddy, Merry said the whole town goes to see the Christmas tree light up. What if I'm the only kid in my class who isn't there?" Wren gave her father a pathetic look.

They were eating dinner and Merry had casually mentioned the tree lighting tonight. The little girl latched on to the idea like a dog with a bone. Merry watched him squirm and felt a little sorry for him. The poor man had been up in the middle of the night with a pregnant cow, helping her through a difficult birth. He'd said both mother and baby were fine, but he looked like the wrath of God.

"Hunter, I can take her. I'll just finish up these dinner dishes and the two of us can head out. You get some rest."

"Does the whole town really go?" he asked.

"I've never taken a head count so I'm sure there are some people who don't attend. But it's always crowded."

Wren shook her head. "It won't be the same with just Merry and me. You have to come, Daddy."

Merry recognized indecision on his face along with the fatigue. When they were exhausted, most people resembled roadkill. Not Hunter Crawford. He made the wrath of God look good. He hadn't shaved and the dark scruff, along with the weariness, somehow made him look brooding and sexier than ever.

Then it occurred to her that his hesitation might be about her. Maybe he wanted alone time with his daughter and was trying to figure out how to say so and not hurt her feelings.

"Wren, maybe your dad wants to take you by himself. Just the two of you. A father/daughter outing."

"No." The little girl put on her stubborn

face like a superhero costume. "Then you would be all alone. And sad."

"Well," he said, "then I guess the three of us are going. It's the most wonderful time of the year. No one is allowed to be sad. Especially my little princess."

"Thank you, Daddy." She hugged him and he kissed the top of her head.

Merry met his gaze. "I'll make you a cup of coffee."

"Thanks." There was a flicker of something in his eyes, probably regret that he wouldn't get some sleep for another couple of hours.

A little while later the three of them pulled into the town hall parking lot. The large pine tree had been set up on the corner of Cedar Street and North Main. They exited the truck and Merry automatically took Wren's hand because there were cars, moving slowly, but she wasn't taking any chances.

On the sidewalk, Wren said, "Daddy, hold my other hand."

"Okay, kiddo."

The little girl turned a happy smile on both of them. "We're all holding hands."

Merry had no idea why but she blushed and her cheeks grew warm. Since it was dark and Hunter couldn't see it, that wasn't necessarily a bad thing, besides a cold wind was blowing. There hadn't been any snow yet, but they still needed to bundle up. She assessed Wren's pink jacket, matching knit hat and fur-lined boots.

"Are you warm enough, sweetie?"

"Yes."

"Are you?" Hunter was looking at Merry.

Could he see the flush on her face? Did he resent her for intruding on this outing? After giving him an out, she wasn't going to dwell on the fact that he hadn't told his daughter no. She had on a cream-colored hat with a pompom, matching mittens and a quilted jacket.

"I'm a little chilly but we'll all huddle around the tree for the lighting and the crush of bodies will block the wind."

It would be lovely if the two of them snuggled up and shared body heat. But that would be a Christmas miracle since there was about as much chance of that happening as Santa actually coming down the chimney.

"I see the tree," Wren shouted. She tugged them along and they moved with a lot of other people all heading in the same direction.

The community tree was situated in a grassy area beside the town hall. They found a spot and eased into it next to an older couple.

"Daddy, I can't see very well."

Merry bent down to the little girl's level and pointed to a break in the bodies. "Look right through there, sweetie."

"I'm tryin', but they keep movin' back and forth. I'm gonna miss the lights."

"I promise you won't," Merry assured her. Knowing Rust Creek Falls, she was sure astronauts on the international space station could probably see this tree when it was lit.

"I'll put you on my shoulders," Hunter said.

"Can you?" Merry tried to gauge his fatigue level. "Are you too tired?"

"Coffee and the cold woke me up." He grinned at her then effortlessly lifted his six-year-old onto his broad shoulders. "How's that, kiddo?"

"Awesome! I can see everything from up here."

Problem solved, except for the part where Merry wanted to sigh at the adorable sight of this swoon-worthy man making sure his daughter had a fulfilling experience. After he'd been up half the night.

They weren't far from a raised platform with a microphone for the town officials—mayor, deputy mayor, sheriff. All of them were assembling now so it shouldn't be too long.

The tall silver-haired woman beside her smiled and leaned close. "What a beautiful family you have."

"Oh, they're—"

"I remember when my daughter was that age and still believed in Santa Claus." She whispered that part so Wren couldn't hear. "Then some little twerp at school told her there was no such thing, before she or her father and I were ready to let that go."

"That's too bad. Kids don't have a filter. And when they learn something that rocks their world, they don't keep it to themselves."

"Isn't that the truth." The woman smiled ruefully. "Not unlike the majority of adults in this town who spread gossip like jam on toast."

"There are plusses and minuses to small-town living," Merry agreed. "That's one of the negatives."

"It's not a deal breaker, though. This is a good place to raise children. Take it from me. My daughter moved away when she got married." She looked at Wren on her father's shoulders. "Don't let your little girl do that."

Before Merry could explain that she was Wren's nanny, there was microphone static. Then Mayor Collin Traub did a sound check. A few years ago the man had won the mayoral election over Nate Crawford, who was a distant relation of the Crawfords at the Ambling A. The man was now the owner of

Maverick Manor, the town's upscale hotel. The current mayor had skillfully guided the town through recovery after the devastating flood and did such a good job, he'd been re-elected by a wide margin.

"Can everyone hear me?" His deep voice traveled well and the crowd murmured that they could. "I'll keep this short because it's cold out here. But you all know that. Let me start off with a public service announcement. Tonight the stores will be open late for you to start, or continue, your holiday shopping.

"Welcome to the Rust Creek Falls annual tree lighting. From now through Christmas there will be lots of holiday events sponsored by the city council. Check the dates and times in the *Rust Creek Falls Gazette* and on the RCF website.

"I want to wish everyone a very merry Christmas and a happy New Year. Now let's get the season going and light up this tree. On the count of five."

The crowd counted along and when they

got to one, green, red, gold and blue lights flashed on giving off a brilliant glow. Ornaments covered the branches and gold-trimmed ribbon wound around the tree. There was a dazzling star on top.

Almost as one voice the crowd said, "Ooh! Wow."

"It looks so pretty. A princess tree. Best one ever!" Wren clapped her mitten-covered hands together. "Don't you think so, Daddy? Aren't you glad you came?"

"I am," he said.

Merry grinned. "So you're not mad at me for mentioning it?"

"Only a little." But his grin said otherwise.

"When are we gonna get our tree?" His daughter looked down at him from her perch on his shoulders. "We hafta get one soon."

"We will. Next week we'll cut one down."

"I can't wait."

The crowd was slowly dispersing and Merry looked for the older woman beside her. She planned to set the record straight about Hunter and Wren not being her family, but the lady had moved away. Part of Merry was glad she didn't have to correct the woman's assumption. Belonging to this family was such a lovely idea. But she wasn't a child who could visit Santa and ask for the gift that meant the most to her.

Hunter set his daughter on the ground. "Thanks for making me do this, princess."

"You're welcome." She smiled at him and the look said she had another request. "Would you thank me for making you get me hot chocolate at Daisy's Donuts?"

He laughed and shook his head. "I don't know. It's a school night. What do you think, Merry?"

She quivered and was pathetically happy just being here with them. If the night went on forever it would be okay with her. "Well, I think that you'll be a little tired at school tomorrow, along with all the other kids who are here. But this only happens once a year."

"Is that a yes?" Wren asked.

"Affirmative," her father teased.

"Does that mean yes?" the little girl demanded.

"It does." Merry held out her hand. "I know you're big, but I need you to hold my hand crossing the street."

"Daddy, too?"

Merry figured he could handle it on his own. He was a grown man. She looked at him and was a little surprised at the intensity on his face. It disappeared when he noticed her watching.

"If he wants," she answered.

"He does," Wren said for him. "Let's all hold hands."

Merry defied anyone to tell this child no. And the three of them crossed North Main Street along with a few other spectators who were walking to Daisy's. A lot of people apparently had the same idea and there were only two tables next to each other that were free. The woman in front of them told her husband and son what to order for her and said she was going to grab one of the tables.

"Good idea." Hunter looked at her. "Why

don't you stake out the last one. Wren and I will get hot chocolate."

"Sounds good."

She sat at a circular table and put her purse and jacket on two other chairs. The woman at the table beside her did the same.

Merry smiled at her. "Good idea to grab these."

"Yeah." She looked thoughtful. "Aren't you an aide at the school?" She didn't wait for an answer. "My son is in sixth grade and I'm sure I've seen you there."

The woman looked vaguely familiar. "Yeah. I work in the primary grades. There are going to be a lot of tired and crabby little ones tomorrow."

"Your little girl doesn't look like she ever gets cranky. And your husband is wrapped around her little finger, I bet." She smiled. "You have a beautiful family."

The words were like a solid whack to the chest, the second one tonight. It was such a wonderful idea, but that's all it was. Just an idea, a notion without a chance of being real.

She smiled and could feel the sadness around the edges. "He's not my husband and that's not my daughter. I'm just her nanny."

"Oh—" The other woman looked distressed. "I'm sorry. I shouldn't have assumed."

Merry didn't hear the rest. A traditional family was everything she'd ever wanted but the dream was not looking good. Since Thanksgiving night Hunter had been different, distant. Oh, he teased and bantered but when their eyes met, she could almost see his barriers securely in place. There hadn't been a glimmer of the raw need she'd seen when he'd almost kissed her. But she must have been mistaken about that.

There was no way he had feelings for her. Not the way she did for him.

Christmas carols played softly in the background. But for her, the most wonderful time of the year wasn't so wonderful.

Chapter Ten

After school the next day Merry met Wren just outside of her classroom for the walk to the truck. Last night's excitement at the town Christmas tree lighting and a fairly substantial sugar high at Daisy's Donuts immediately after made it way past bedtime when the little girl was finally asleep. Merry had expected to collect a tired, cranky and out-of-sorts child that afternoon, but that's not what happened.

"Merry!" Wren ran over and was practically jumping up and down. Clearly she was excited about something. "You'll never guess what happened."

She made an exaggeration of studying the happy little face. "Well, I'm guessing it's something pretty fantastic judging by that deliriously happy smile."

"It is. I got a big part in the Christmas play." She clapped her hands together. "It's going to be at the community center and my teacher said almost everyone in town comes to watch."

"Oh, sweetie, that's wonderful." She bent down to hug her. "What part did you get?"

"I'm going to play Rudolph's best friend, Dancer."

"Awesome."

"It's the second-biggest part and there are a lot of lines to learn." The smile dimmed just a little.

"I can help you with that, sweetie. And you have a really good memory. That's probably why your teacher picked you. Learning your lines will be a piece of cake. You'll see."

"We better go home so I can start."

"Okay." When the little girl trustingly slipped her hand into Merry's, there was a definite tug on Merry's heart. She hoped she was creating a positive difference in this young life. That would go a long way toward making this hopeless crush on Hunter Crawford mean something.

Hand in hand, they weaved through the crowd of children who'd just been dismissed from class and walked to the lot where Merry's old truck was parked. She took the pink backpack and set it on the back seat, then lifted Wren up. Without a running board it was next to impossible for six-year-old little legs to breach the distance.

"Hop on into your car seat, sweetie."

"You always say that."

"Because I always want you to be safe."

"You always say that, too." Wren spontaneously hugged her.

That gave Merry's heart another delicious tug and she squeezed the small body close for a moment. "I'm very glad to know you listen to what I say."

"I do."

"Good." She pulled away and winked. "Now, make sure you—"

"Buckle yourself in," Wren finished.

They were both laughing as Merry closed the truck door. She walked around and opened the driver's side and climbed behind the wheel. "Okay, let's get you home. Are you hungry?"

"Yes. Can I have peanut butter on crackers and some apple slices? I like the way you cut them up into skinny pieces."

"Of course. That sounds like a very nutritious snack. And we have everything. I don't have to stop at the store before we leave town."

She put her key in the ignition and started the engine, then backed out of her space and headed slowly for the exit onto South Main Street. She made a right turn to go north out of Rust Creek Falls toward the ranch.

It was awfully quiet in the passenger area. "Everything okay back there?"

"Yes. I can't wait to tell Daddy about the play."

"He's going to be pretty excited and very proud of you." She glanced in the rearview mirror and noted an uneasy look on that sweet face. "Something wrong?"

"My teacher said for the play the whole class gets to help make fake snow out of construction paper because when Santa and the reindeer land the sleigh, it slides on snow."

"Good. Then the whole class will feel like they're part of the play. Everyone makes an important contribution. No one gets left out. That's the meaning of Rudolph the Red-Nosed Reindeer's story."

"That's what my teacher said."

Merry noted that she still sounded a little concerned. "What's really bothering you, honey?"

"In Texas there wasn't any snow where we lived but Daddy said Santa is magic and would come anyway because there isn't snow everywhere he goes."

"Your dad is right."

"But before we moved here to Montana he told me there would be snow by December and there isn't any."

"That's true. It has been unseasonably warm this year," Merry admitted. "But look at that sky. If those aren't snow clouds I don't know what are."

"I hope so. I'm so tired of waitin'." There was a whole lot of emotion in those words.

"If it's not a problem for Santa, why is it so important?"

"Mistlesnow."

"What now?" Merry asked.

"When it starts to snow, you make a wish and it will come true."

"That's sweet. I never heard that before. What a lovely idea."

"It didn't snow for Uncle Finn and Aunt Avery's wedding. And it got cold here, too, but there's nothing. I've been waitin' and waitin'. I never saw it snow before. And I can't hardly wait to make a wish."

"Well, I've lived in Montana for a while now and it's snowed every winter. And I'm pretty sure it's in the weather forecast for today. So, just keep an eye on that sky."

"Okay."

Merry glanced in the rearview mirror again and saw the little girl staring eagerly out the truck window. She smiled and was charmed yet again by this special child. Obviously she had her mother's DNA but she'd been raised solely by her father. That made him a pretty special man. Clearly he had so much to give. It was a darn shame that Hunter was so closed off and that made her sad.

A few minutes later she made the turn onto the road that led to the Ambling A Ranch. She drove about a mile in and the cluster of buildings came into view. Moments later she parked in front of the log cabin. Hunter was standing on the covered porch, which wasn't a surprise, but Merry's heart skipped a beat at the sight of him. That wasn't a surprise either. The same thing happened nearly every day because he was almost always waiting to make sure his daughter got safely home so he could hear about her day. After that he went back to whatever job he'd been doing.

He stepped off the porch and lifted a hand in greeting. She sighed a little at the intensely masculine sight of him with his black Stetson pulled low on his forehead and his sheepskin jacket accentuating broad shoulders. He moved to the truck's rear passenger door to lift out his little girl.

"How was your day, kiddo?"

"Daddy, it was the best day ever." She told him all about the play and her part. "Merry is gonna help me remember my lines."

He met her gaze. "Thank you."

"No need to thank me. I'd be happy to do it even if it wasn't part of my responsibilities."

"Still, I appreciate it." There was gratitude in his expression along with something hot and intense.

The look lasted only a moment before the spark flickered and was firmly extinguished. What a shame. But she understood. Life had kicked him in the teeth. Who could blame him for protecting himself and his daughter?

"You're welcome. Because, it has to be said, your child can be so difficult." Since she was the exact opposite of that, the teasing words made him smile. "Seriously, I should pay you. She is a joy to be around."

"Yeah, she's a pretty great kid. I think I'll keep her—"

"Look!" Wren pointed at a few fluffy white flakes drifting down from the sky, then held her palm up to catch one. "Is it snow?"

"Yes," Merry said.

"You were right. Merry said it would snow today." The little girl hugged her. "Mistles-now. Quick. Make a wish."

Wren closed her eyes and there was a look of fierce concentration on her face. Merry wished for the first thing that popped into her head. Hunter just looked confused.

"Mistlesnow," Merry said. "It's a new thing for me, too. When it first starts to snow, you make a wish. I'm told it will come true."

"Then I wish for the snow to stop," he said. "I've got work to do."

"Daddy, you can't say your wish out loud," his daughter scolded. "It won't come true."

"My bad." He shrugged those impossibly broad shoulders. "I'll make another one."

"Too late," Wren told him. "You only get one wish."

Merry's eyebrows lifted. "Apparently she's the mistlesnow police."

Hunter laughed and for the third time that day she felt a tug on her heart. He didn't smile nearly often enough, so the bonus of that cheerful sound was particularly satisfying. On the down side, the brooding man was gone, replaced by this smiling one who could so easily make her weak in the knees. A memory of the kiss that never was went through her mind and she sighed with disappointment. She just knew it would have been the best kiss she'd ever had.

Even a mistlesnow wish wouldn't be powerful enough to confirm her suspicions. It was no match for his defenses. She was grateful for Wren's rules of keeping a wish to yourself. Hers had been about Hunter, an involuntary yearning to be with him that had popped into her mind. Saying it out loud would have been humiliating.

But that was nothing compared to the pain of wanting something she could never have.

"There are a couple more things I need to run by you, Dad." Hunter had been pacing in his father's office up at the big ranch house. Wilder was here for this meeting, too. "I want to increase the herd."

Max leaned back in his cushy leather chair and steepled his fingers. "Are you sure about that, son?"

"Yes, sir, I am. I know we started this operation small because of the move. The plan was to increase slowly. Grazing management is more cost effective with a bigger herd. By that, I mean it's quicker and more efficient to check on, say, five hundred cows in one herd than a hundred cows in five herds."

His father looked at Wilder, who was sprawled in one of the chairs in front of the big desk. "Do you agree with your brother?"

"Yes, sir. He's the one with that fancy college degree in ranching from Texas A&M. But it's just common sense. Increase profits without a big investment in overhead."

Max nodded. "Okay then. Go for it."

"Okay. I'll start the process." Hunter grinned.

It always felt good to have his father's approval. Max Crawford didn't become successful by making stupid decisions. His personal life was less praiseworthy and the six brothers had paid a price for that. But Hunter wasn't going there. He still had to finish this meeting.

"Also," he said, "I'm going to look for a used baler. More cows means more hay to feed them in the winter."

"What about buying new?" Wilder asked.

"A used one is cheaper. That keeps down the cost of expanding the herd."

"What if it needs repairs?" his brother wanted to know.

"You and I have learned to make repairs. But if something happens that we can't handle, there's a local guy. Brendan Tanner. He's an ex-marine who's supposed to be really good at fixing machinery."

"How do you know this?" Wilder gave him a look that said "you've been holding out." "No offense, bro, but you're not very friendly. You make hermits look social."

"I'm social. I just talk to different people than you." And by that he meant women. His brother went out of his way to talk to them. Hunter didn't. He preferred chatting with local ranchers about cattle prices and machinery. "But I do get around."

Like Thanksgiving night when he'd almost kissed Merry. The regret of not doing that got bigger every time he saw her. And the temptation to follow through with what he'd started was becoming nearly impossible to resist. Then he saw his brother studying him with questions in his eyes and forced himself back into the moment.

"I ran into Paddy O'Reilly in town. He's a local rancher and Brendan is his daughter's husband."

"I think all your plans look good." Max nodded. "And I've carefully considered the spreadsheets you gave me and the bottom line is impressive. I think you should allocate some funds to start fixing up your house."

"Do this place first," he said, looking around the office. The house was livable but needed updating, especially the kitchen, according to his sister-in-law, Lily. "My house is fine."

"I know. But Wren is growing up. She'll be wanting to have her friends over before you know it," Max pointed out.

Hunter didn't want to think about her getting older. That meant more freedom, independence, social situations where he couldn't always be there to make sure she was safe. But, if she felt comfortable inviting her friends to the house, Merry would be there to supervise. Or not. She was a beautiful woman and wouldn't necessarily stay on forever.

From experience he knew that men plan

and God laughs. He couldn't count on anything being the way he wanted it to be.

Still, he would rather have his daughter socializing here on the ranch. "You have a point, Dad."

"I do?" Max's eyebrows rose.

"Don't look so surprised," Wilder needled.

"Hard not to. I get more pushback than agreement from you boys."

"We have our reasons." Hunter rested a hip on the corner of the desk.

"I know." Max's voice was deep, serious. "There's been some hard knocks in this family. But lately you've got more of a spring in your step."

"Me?" Hunter asked.

"Yeah, I'm looking at you." The twinkle was back in his father's eyes.

"I've noticed that, too," Wilder said. "You've been much easier to work with lately."

"You're both full of it." Hunter glared at his brother. "And I've always been a sweetheart of a guy to work with."

His younger brother laughed, a mocking sound. "Are you serious? You're like a ticked-off grizzly bear, and that's on a good day. But recently you've mellowed."

Max nodded his agreement. "I think this move to Montana has been good for you. A change of scene, not just for you, but Wren, too. It's been just the thing to get you out of the rut you've been in."

"I wasn't in a rut," Hunter protested. "Working and raising a daughter are what I do."

"That's called a rut," his brother said.

"What do you know? Your life is work and women. That's what you call a rut," Hunter countered.

Wilder shifted in the chair and met his father's gaze. "Now that you mention it, Dad, his attitude adjusted pretty recently. Right around the time Finn and Avery got married."

"Ah." Max nodded knowingly. "That's when you hired Merry Matthews full time.

By the way, how are things working out with her?"

"Wren loves her. And knowing she's there taking care of my daughter gives me peace of mind." Knowing she was under his roof at night gave him no peace at all. It drove him crazy. She slept just down the hall and he was tied up in knots from the longing to go to her, hold her. And more.

"But is it just about Wren?" Max asked.

Since when could his father read minds? Or figure out what someone else was feeling? Hunter was starting to feel like that ticked-off grizzly his brother had called him. "What do you mean?"

"Merry is obviously wonderful with my granddaughter. But she's also quite a lovely young woman. Smart, sweet and pretty. I can't help wondering if she isn't—well— making you merry."

Hunter narrowed his gaze on his father. "This has to be said. It makes me skittish when I have your approval. Especially about a woman."

"He has a point, Dad." Wilder glanced at him then back to their father. "You have to admit you're not the best judge of character where women are concerned."

Hunter recalled Max admitting that he'd done some things to manipulate their mother, controlling moves to get her to stay. Misguided love could best describe what they'd had. But the woman had given up on her kids.

"My brother is saying you chose a woman who walked out and left six boys motherless. And he has a point."

"You'll never know how much I regret what happened with me and your mother." Max really did look sorry. "I made mistakes. But I can't change the past. My concern is for your futures. Four of my sons have settled down. It's just you two left to take care of."

"It is what it is, Dad. Just leave it alone."

"Seriously, Hunter?" His brother laughed but there was no humor in it. "Have you met our father? When did he not stick his nose in our business thinking he knew best?"

"There is that." Hunter braced for a blistering retort from his father and was surprised when it didn't come.

"I deserve that. You may not believe this, but everything I do is out of love for you boys." Max sighed a little sadly. "But you're men now. All grown up. And I can see how what I've done wrong has affected you. I'm going to fix it, though. I will see all of my sons happily settled down with families of their own, or die trying."

Wilder jumped out of the chair as if a snake had bitten him in the backside. Something about the sheer force of will in their father's expression had obviously spooked him. That and the fact that his four older brothers had fallen like dominoes and were married.

"I'm good, Dad. Really," Wilder said. "Don't waste your time on me. I'm perfectly happy playing the field. Settling down is not my game plan. I mean, can you really see me as a father?" He shook his head and shuddered. "Not gonna happen. So—and I mean this in the best possible way—back off."

Max just smiled.

That made Wilder even more nervous. "I assume this meeting is over. It is for me anyway. The horses must need feeding. Chores are waiting. I'm out of here."

Hunter watched as his brother couldn't get out of the room fast enough. "Good luck with him, Dad."

"I'm not worried. He'll come around."

Then he noticed that his father's determined gaze was trained on him. Suddenly he understood how cornered his brother had felt. They both said he'd been happier since Merry had come to work for him. Their imaginations were working overtime. He hadn't changed.

"Look, Dad, don't analyze me. Wren and I are good. She loves school. By the way, she's in the Christmas play and excited about that. She's looking forward to Christmas. If my daughter is happy, I'm happy. It's as simple as that."

"If you say so, son." Max looked like the cat that swallowed the canary. He wasn't buying this.

Hunter felt as if every time he opened his mouth to make the case for his recent positive mood change, he actually made his father's case for Merry being at the heart of it. He wouldn't let that be true, even if it killed him. And now he was starting to think like Max Crawford, who'd admitted to manipulating his sons to get them settled down.

It was time to follow his little brother's example and beat a hasty retreat. "Speaking of Christmas, I need to get my little girl a tree to decorate."

"If I know my granddaughter, she's going to want her nanny to come along," Max pointed out with some satisfaction.

The man wasn't wrong, Hunter thought. And if he was being completely honest with himself, he wouldn't mind Merry's company either, and not just to look out for Wren.

Her smiling face seemed to make everything better. But neither wild horses nor his father could drag that admission out of him.

Chapter Eleven

Merry felt awful about asking Hunter for the evening off. He'd just returned to the house after a meeting with his father and said something about taking Wren to chop down a Christmas tree. But her house was closing escrow very soon, and she needed to pack up what was going into storage, then clean out, toss out or give away what was left. Hunter had generously agreed to her request. Since his daughter had said she wanted Merry to go, they'd put off the excursion until the following day. That sweet little girl's words made Merry's eyes well up with tears every time she thought about it.

Now she was in the kitchen along with a stack of boxes she'd gotten from Crawford's General Store, and bubble wrap and a tape dispenser in order to securely seal the box flaps.

Shaking her head, she looked around at the cupboards and knickknacks. Fortunately it was a small kitchen, but still... "This is going to be the worst," she said aloud.

The doorbell rang and she was grateful for the momentary reprieve. She'd asked Zoey to give her a hand, and her friend was standing on the porch with more boxes, flattened for easier transport.

"I am so glad to see you." Merry hugged her friend. "So much to do, so little time. I'm suddenly feeling very overwhelmed."

"Don't worry. We'll get this done." There was a confident, reassuring look in her friend's blue eyes.

Merry really needed that. "It's going to be emotional, too."

"I know." Zoey gave her a hard squeeze then let go. "So, what are we doing first?"

"Kitchen." Merry took half the boxes and led the way to the back of the house. After leaning the stack against one of the dinette chairs, she said, "This is going to be the biggest job. After dad died I cleaned out his room and donated his clothes. Most of his tools sold in the garage sale. That leaves the furniture and my things. And the kitchen."

"Let's get down to business," Zoey said.

Working together, they wrapped dishware, then arranged it snugly in a box to minimize breakage. When it was full, Merry sealed the top and labeled it with a black Sharpie.

"Now we have to box those pots and pans, and that cast iron skillet that was my mother's."

"My mom has one, too. She swears by it." Zoey opened a cupboard next to the stove and studied the contents—a lot of spices. "Are you sure you don't want to bring some of this stuff out to the ranch? You're cooking for Hunter and Wren, right?"

"Yes."

"Might be nice to have some of the cookware you're used to. And these bottles of spices won't do well in storage."

"I hadn't thought about that." She mulled it over and nodded. "It's a good idea. I'll run it by Hunter."

"I'll get some of the flat boxes ready for packing the other stuff," Zoey said. "Speaking of the ranch, how is it going? Living there, I mean."

"The timing of it all couldn't have worked out better," Merry said, ruefully surveying the open cupboard. There were things inside she used only once a year and had forgotten about. She wrapped up a gravy boat and handed it to her friend. "At least I don't have to worry right away about where I'm going to live."

"Do you think this ranch arrangement is permanent?"

"Is anything?" Merry was the poster girl for change. "Right now Wren seems really happy that I'm there."

"And her father?"

"What about him?" Besides the fact that his deep voice sent shivers down her spine and made her tingle in places she'd never tingled before.

Zoey gave her a "duh" look. "Is he happy you're there?"

"He hasn't said he's not." Technically that was true, but she saw looks on his face when he didn't know she was watching. Dark expressions that made her wonder if he was questioning the decision to hire her.

Zoey took a wrapped glass and set it in the box. "I know you're fiercely independent and all that, but you don't ever have to worry about a place to live. My mom considers you another daughter. We will always have room for you."

"Oh, Zo—" She blinked at the moisture suddenly in her eyes. "You're gonna make me cry."

"Don't you dare. Or I'll start." She sniffled. "Now hand me another glass."

"I appreciate the offer more than I can tell you. But—" She shrugged. "It's all good."

"Then why do I keep reading between the lines? It's all good—right now. It's fine—but…"

"I don't mean to imply that," Merry said. "It's just that life has given me more than one lesson about how things can change from one day to the next."

"Yeah. That's something we all need to keep in mind." Zoey studied her carefully. "It's just that I can't shake the feeling there's something not the same about you."

The only difference was working for Hunter and fighting the attraction that stubbornly refused to go away. But she was shocked to find out that it showed and hoped with every fiber of her being that Hunter wasn't as observant as her friend. She had to sell the pretense that nothing about her had changed, starting now.

"Obviously I'm different," she started. "My dad died and I sold the house." She wrapped up four small custard dishes. "That would change anyone."

"I understand that, honey." Her friend looked sympathetic. "But what I see didn't start until you began working at the ranch."

"And don't forget that I have another job. That makes two. So I've got a lot on my plate. No pun intended," she said, handing over a platter.

Zoey grinned, then her expression faded into a thoughtful look. "You worked two jobs when you filled in as clerical staff for your dad, but I never saw you like this."

"Exhausted?" Merry wished her friend would just drop the subject. Talking about her feelings was a waste of breath because it wouldn't make Hunter return them. "So, what you're really saying is that I look really bad."

"Oh, honey, not at all. In fact, just the opposite. Every time you mention Hunter your eyes light up. There's a sort of glow about you."

"Just so you know," she said wryly, "I'm not pregnant."

"That never crossed my mind. But, trust me, I never saw you look like this before you started working at the Ambling A." Then Zoey's gaze narrowed. "Come to think of it, I noticed a difference when you came over to the house to try on dresses for the wedding. Right after you met Hunter for the first time."

Love at first sight? Not if she could help it. But it was time to come clean. Zoey was her BFF and their relationship was based on honesty and support. The least Merry could do was be honest now.

"He impresses me, Zoey. I respect him a lot. He's such a good father and it can't have been easy. His wife died a few days after Wren was born. Complications from child-birth."

"Oh, my God." Her friend's eyes widened. "That poor man. And sweet little Wren without a mom—"

"Yeah. I can't even imagine what it was

like to never know your mother." She pulled the last couple of glasses out of the cupboard. "He had his father and brothers. They're great. I spent time with them at the wedding and Thanksgiving. Four of them—"

"Are married. I know. So do all the single women in Rust Creek Falls. Trust me, we're doing the math. We can subtract. There are only two eligible Crawford bachelors left. Three if you count their father."

"Oh, brother." Merry rolled her eyes. "But Hunter is a package deal, what with having a daughter. The thing is, you can't help falling in love with that little girl."

"Are you in love with Hunter, too?"

"That would be stupid," she protested.

Her friend slid a half-filled box closer to where Merry was working by the stove. "But stupid doesn't make it not true."

"I don't have time for that. And, seriously? You're helping pack up my house. The one I just sold. My life is nothing but one big challenge. I don't need more." She turned away to empty out a cupboard. "I have two jobs and soon I'm going to be taking online classes again to finish up my teaching credentials."

"Again, Mer, none of that means you're not falling for him."

"Well, I'm not." *Please, God, let that be true.* "I admire him. I like him. But love? Hardly. If anything besides my boss, he's a friend. And I'm grateful to him."

"For?"

"After being dumped by a selfish jerk, he's shown me that there are still good men around."

"So..." Zoey was giving her the "I'm seeing hearts all around you" look. "Love is a possibility?"

"Not a chance."

"Why do you say that?"

Merry hated to crush her friend's romantic notions, but the BFF code of honesty was carved in stone. "In so many ways he's shown he's one of the good guys. With his brothers and his father. But mostly with his devotion to his daughter. He's completely wrapped up in her. Unfortunately, he's so focused on being one of the good guys, there's no time or room in his life for anyone else."

"That's too bad." Zoey nodded a little sadly.

Usually talking to her friend made her feel better. Not this time. Saying the words out loud was like a stone on her heart. But something else bothered her even more. If Zoey could see she felt something, it was possible Hunter could, too. And soon she had to go back to her job at the ranch and hope he didn't notice her eyes light up when she looked at him.

After school the next day Merry was in the truck with Hunter and Wren, driving to Fall Mountain to cut down a fresh pine tree for Christmas. There wasn't a cloud in the sky, and she was wearing dark glasses to protect her eyes from the sun's glare. Or was it to have some protection against giving away her feelings?

She glanced at the man in the driver's seat

and actually felt her heart skip a beat. This stretch of road was flat and straight and he was in control of the truck with one hand on the steering wheel. What in the world made that such a sexy look? If she could figure that out, it could be the key to controlling her attraction.

He looked over and met her gaze. "Everything okay?"

"Fine." She cleared her throat. "I just wanted to thank you for putting this off a day so that I can tag along."

"Wren insisted you be here." The subtext was that he was a no vote on her presence, but because he was devoted to his daughter she got what she wanted. "But it turned out to be a good thing because I got a chance to dig through a bunch of moving boxes that are still unpacked and find the stuff for the tree."

"Then it's a win-win."

He nodded. "Speaking of moving boxes... Did you make progress on your packing?"

"Yes. My friend Zoey helped." She could

see they were going uphill now and there were more trees.

"Are we there yet, Daddy?" Wren piped up from the back seat.

He looked in the rearview mirror and smiled. "I thought you were asleep."

"Nope. I can hardly wait to pick out my tree. A real tree."

"We usually have an artificial one," he explained. "This year she wore me down. Someone in town told me about a spot up here on the mountain where the sun hits just right to make the pines full and fragrant."

"I sure hope we find it pretty soon." Wren's voice was just south of a whine.

"We're getting there," he said.

Halfway up the mountain they reached an unpaved road and he made a left onto it, then drove slowly until coming to a stop in front of a thick grove of trees. There were stumps scattered among them that looked freshly cut, as if they'd recently been chopped down by others who'd come before them. Patches of snow from the recent storm managed to survive in shady areas beneath thick branches where the sun didn't touch them.

Hunter turned off the engine and announced, "We're here."

"Yay!" Wren quickly freed herself from her seat belt, opened her door and jumped out of the truck.

Before she could race off, Merry called out, "Stay where I can see you, sweetie."

"Oh, man." The little girl was impatient. "You guys are too slow."

"It would be easy to get lost in all these trees," she explained firmly. "I need to watch you."

Hunter chuckled. "And that's another reason why I didn't mind waiting for you to be available. I'm glad you're here to be the enforcer."

"You'd handle it if I wasn't."

"Yeah. But I'm glad you are."

His voice was warm and smooth, two parts gravel, one part velvet. Her breath caught for a moment but she managed to say, "Two pairs of eyes are better than one."

"Daddy, Merry, come on," Wren said impatiently.

"We're coming."

They exited the truck and Hunter grabbed a long-handled ax from the bed. Merry stood beside Wren, wanting to take her hand. She'd seen too many news stories about people lost for days in the wilderness and surviving by eating bugs and drinking water from tree leaves. As far as she could tell, pine needles were not an especially good receptacle for liquid. But the need to give this child a little independence won out over her protective instinct.

"Do you see anything you like, honey?" Hunter asked his daughter.

"This one." The girl pointed to the tree beside her.

He nodded. "Not bad. But don't you want to look around?"

"Can we?"

"Of course," he said.

They walked a short way, assessing the height, fullness and symmetry of different pines that caught their interest. Merry noticed Hunter was subtly guiding them in a pattern that always kept the truck in sight. That told her they were on the same wavelength about getting lost.

"What about this one, Wren?" Merry pointed out a pine tree that was a foot or two taller than Hunter. Using his height as a gauge, she judged that it would be prefect for the cabin's living room.

The little girl walked around the perimeter, giving it a critical once-over. "Does it have holes?"

By "holes" she meant places that were less full than others. Merry walked around it. "I don't see any."

"Daddy, what do you think?"

He did the same circuit and nodded. "This could be the one, kiddo. Just say the word."

She grinned happily. "I like it."

"Okay, then. You stand out of the way with Merry and I'll chop it down." He pointed to a spot and the two of them obediently walked over and stood there. Then he took a whack at the trunk on the opposite side of the tree from them.

Merry just had to ask. "Have you ever done this before?"

The look he gave her was amused. "Nervous?"

"No. Yes. Maybe."

"Here's how it's done." He indicated the mark he'd made on the trunk and started cutting on a forty-five degree angle. "I'll give it a thinner, less angled wedge, a few inches above the first cut. It will fall away from you. Trust me."

Trust was hard for her, but that was emotionally speaking. He would never risk his daughter getting hurt. Watching his powerful swings, she was distracted and way more interested in the masculine display of manliness. He looked so hot in his Stetson and sheepskin jacket. If there was a better word to describe him, she didn't know it. The man appealed to her in a very big way, on every level she could think of.

He came around and did his thing on the

other side of the tree and it fell exactly where he'd said it would.

"Timber." He grinned and his grin said, "I told you so."

"Nice job, Daddy." The little girl ran over and hugged him. "Can I carry the ax back to the truck? It's not too heavy, I promise."

There was no way she could know that since Merry was almost positive her father would not ever have let her touch the thing.

"No, honey. It's really sharp," he said, confirming her guess.

"I won't touch that part." She gave him puppy dog eyes.

On top of that look, Merry could see a lot of stubborn sliding into Wren's expression. She decided a diversion would be good. "Is anyone else cold? I sure am. If we hurry home, I can make hot chocolate." She looked at the little girl and asked, "With whipped cream or marshmallows?"

"Can I squirt the whipped cream right out of the can into my mouth?" Wren began the familiar negotiation. "Cuz you don't usually let me."

"Hmm. You drive a hard bargain. But since it's tree cutting day, I think we can make an exception."

"Okay." Wren put her hand into Merry's.

"That sounds like a plan." Hunter gave her a thankful look, then rested the ax handle on his shoulder with one hand. He grabbed the trunk of the fallen tree with the other and dragged it back to the truck.

The sun was low in the sky and getting ready to disappear behind the mountain when they got back to the ranch. Another distraction was needed when the little girl wanted to jump right into decorating and was told the tree needed to be hosed off to get rid of bugs and any other critters lurking in the branches.

Then it had to dry because they couldn't bring a wet tree into the house. Merry knew Wren was hungry and tired, which could easily cause a meltdown and spoil her holiday experience. For their first Christmas in

Montana, in this cabin, Merry was determined not to let anything mar the memories.

"I have an idea," she said.

"What?" Wren's expression was part pout, part suspicion.

"While the tree is drying, we'll have something to eat. I made chicken soup and we'll have a little salad. You can have your hot chocolate—"

"With whipped cream?"

"Of course. That will give you energy for decorating and make the waiting go faster."

Wren thought that over and finally nodded. "Okay."

"I'll go wash off the tree." On his way out the kitchen door, Hunter stopped and said so only she could hear, "You're the child whisperer. That was pure genius."

"Thanks."

The compliment made her feel warm and gooey inside, but their faces were inches apart. She could feel his breath on her cheek. With very little effort she could touch her lips to his. And she wanted that so badly, there was an ache inside her the size of Montana itself. Something hot flashed in his eyes, something that looked like regret, just before he moved away and out the door.

After dinner Merry fast-talked the little girl into a quick bath before decorating, while her dad brought in the tree and set it in the stand. The lights were strung by the time they came downstairs.

"Let the decorating begin," Hunter said.

The three of them carefully placed brightly colored ornaments then draped a garland. He easily lifted his daughter up to set the angel on the top.

"Perfect," he said, just before he put her down. "Just one more thing to do. I'm going to plug it in."

When he did, the white lights went on and Wren's look of wonder was priceless. "It's the best Christmas tree ever," she said reverently.

Hunter came over to stand beside them. "Looks pretty good. You picked out a winner, kiddo."

"It smells wonderful," Merry said. "Like a pine forest."

"Best day ever." Wren leaned against her and yawned.

It was the sign Merry had been waiting for. "Wow, look how late it is. We've been so busy I didn't even notice that it's past your bedtime, sweetie."

"Okay." The little girl headed for the stairs without being told.

Hunter met her gaze and his was full of surprise. "Wow. No pushback. That's amazing."

"Not really. Fresh air. Excitement. Activity. I'm surprised she held out this long."

They tucked her into bed and Merry tiptoed downstairs to look at the tree again while Hunter read the nightly story. Five minutes later he joined her.

"How did you get away with skimming that book?" she asked.

"I didn't have to. She fell asleep. Out cold in the first two minutes."

"She's a trooper, but it was obvious that she was worn out."

"By the way," he said. "Thank you for today. You're so good with her. Things could have gone sideways so many times, but because of you they didn't."

"Happy to help." She wanted to add that it was what he was paying her for, but she didn't. This was a moment and she didn't want to go there.

"The tree looks good." He crossed his arms over his chest.

"Beautiful." She was feeling wistful and just a little sorry for herself. When she was busy, it was easy to forget that she was facing a move and a lot of uncertainty about her future. But for now she had a roof over her head. "Thank you."

"For what?" He sounded surprised.

"If I wasn't here, I wouldn't have a tree this year."

"Because of the move," he said.

She nodded. "I have to be out before Christmas. All my things are packed and will go into storage with the furniture. I have to figure out the logistics of making that happen."

"You're going to need help. Let me know when and I'll give you a hand."

"I couldn't ask you—"

"You didn't ask. I volunteered. I won't take no for an answer. And I'll bring Wilder. The two of us should be enough muscle to get the job done."

"Really?" She stared up at him. "You'd do that for me?"

"Of course. It's the least I can do to thank you for going above and beyond the call of duty with Wren."

Merry had worried so much about how she was going to pull off this move. She'd felt so alone since her dad died and even before that. Caring for him by herself when he was so ill had been isolating and scary. To have someone take half the load now was such an incredible relief.

"Oh, Hunter—"

Happiness bubbled up and she couldn't

stop herself. She threw her arms around him. "I can't thank you enough."

He went completely still and she instantly realized she'd made a huge mistake. Employees didn't generally hug their boss. She'd just crossed the line and somehow she had to fix this.

She took a step back. "I'm so sorry—"

"Merry, I—"

His eyes went hot and dark just before he pulled her back into his arms and kissed her.

Chapter Twelve

Merry was completely swept away. She'd never expected to feel this way. Not ever. But wrapped in Hunter's arms, the warmth of his body, the feel of his mouth on hers was more powerful than she'd imagined. And so was his kiss. It was real, solid and it was truly happening. She slid her arms around his neck, loving the sensation of his big hand moving gently up and down her back.

Heat poured through her and she ran her fingers through his hair at the nape of his neck. His breathing was uneven and she could feel his heart pounding as hard as her own. When he stopped kissing her she thought he was just coming up for air. But that wasn't it.

He stepped away, then took her hands in his and squeezed them gently before letting go. "Merry, I'm—"

"Don't you dare say you're sorry."

The strong fragrant pine scent surrounded them and the glow from the Christmas tree highlighted his surprise. "Okay. Then I'll just say this is all my fault."

"Fault?" She blinked at him. "You kissed me. I kissed you back. Fault implies there's something wrong with that."

He rubbed a shaking hand over his face. "I shouldn't have done that."

"If someone has to take responsibility for something, an argument could be made that it should be me. Because I hugged you first." She glared at him. "And, for the record, I'm not sorry. At all."

"I'm not asking you to be. Your caring nature is one of the qualities I like most. It's why you're so good with my daughter. And you shouldn't have to change that." He let out a long breath. "But I need to maintain a higher standard."

"So you're ashamed of this?"

"I'm disappointed in myself for not being stronger."

She stared at him for several moments. "Should I be flattered or insulted?"

"For God's sake, Merry. You work for me. I don't want to put you in a compromising position."

So he was being noble. "That's really sweet."

"No." He shook his head. "It's the right thing to do."

"So this compromising position…" She couldn't believe she was going to do this. But some instinct warned that if she turned her back now she would regret it for the rest of her life. Instead, she closed the space between them and looked up, needing him to see in her eyes everything she was feeling. There was no trying to hide it now. "It's not a compromising position if that's where I want to be."

He resisted for a second or two and then his face softened. "So, that's a yes?"

She laughed and took his hand in hers, intertwining their fingers. "Affirmative."

Without another word they walked upstairs to his bedroom and closed the door behind them. Hunter flipped a switch on the wall and a nightstand lamp went on.

Merry had no doubts about this but that didn't mean she wasn't nervous. Gripping his hand a little tighter she said, "I feel it might be a good idea to manage your expectations—"

"Have you changed your mind? It's okay—"

"No. I'm very sure. It's just—" She couldn't quite meet his gaze. "I haven't had a lot of experience."

He nudged her chin up until she met his gaze. There was a gentle smile curving the corners of his mouth. "I'm the one who should be warning you about expectations.

But I do have protection even though it's been a long time for me."

That hadn't occurred to her and she was grateful he had thought about it. "Okay."

Something must have shown on her face because any trace of teasing disappeared from his. "That's not why I want you. This is not something I take lightly."

She smiled. "I wouldn't be here if I thought you did. So, let's turn down the bed."

She walked to the far side and they dragged the top of the comforter to the foot of the bed, then folded it over one more time. Hunter opened the nightstand drawer and took out a square packet, setting it aside. Never letting her gaze stray from his, she knelt on the mattress. He did the same on the other side and they came together in the center of the king-size bed.

He reached for the hem of her sweater and she lifted her arms, letting him drag it up and over her head. She tugged his shirt from the waistband of his worn jeans and unsnapped the closures, one by one. Before she was halfway done he pulled on the sides of the shirt, opening all the snaps before quickly shrugging it off.

With trembling hands, Merry unhooked her bra and he brushed the straps off her shoulders, then tossed the scrap of white somewhere. With the light behind him, she couldn't see the expression on his face, but his breathing was ragged and his hands shook a little when he touched her.

He cupped her breasts in his palms and caressed them with his thumbs. "You're beautiful—"

"You make me feel beautiful."

"Merry—"

He sucked in a breath when she put her hands over his to hold them in place on her bare skin. He kissed her then, and pulled her against him, tunneling his fingers into her hair. His chest was wide and muscular and the dusting of hair scraped her skin in the best possible way. She opened her mouth to him and their tongues dueled as he explored while she did the same to him.

The room was filled with the sounds of their harsh breathing. Then she reached for the buckle on his belt as he undid the button on her jeans. The rest of their clothes came off and were tossed carelessly aside. He settled on the mattress and pulled her down on top of him. Finally she was in his arms, bare skin to bare skin.

Rolling her to the side, he slid his hand down her back, over the curve of her waist, and came to rest on her hip for a moment. He squeezed gently then moved his palm between her legs and slid one finger inside. Her muscles contracted as an ache cracked open and the need to be filled grew unbearable. A yearning that she'd had almost from the moment they met became too much to resist. Her hips arched toward him, telling him without words what she was asking for.

He moved away and grabbed the condom, then put it on. Seconds later he was kissing her again, angling his mouth over hers, trailing kisses over her cheek, jaw and neck. Taking his weight on his forearms, he covered her body with his own and gently nudged her legs apart. When he slowly entered her, she lifted her hips to meet him and take him deeper inside.

She touched his broad shoulders, slid her palms over his muscular biceps and met him thrust for thrust. Her breathing grew shallow and harsh as he took her higher and higher, right to the edge. After hovering there for a moment an explosion of pleasure ripped through her and she trembled from the force of it.

"I've got you," he whispered against her hair as he held her.

When she came back together again, she smiled up at him and said, "I've got you, too."

She wrapped her legs around his waist, holding him to her as he started to move again. He thrust once, slowly, then increased the pace, finding their rhythm together and igniting her desire once again. And then he groaned and tensed. Reaching her own climax once more, she held him close and they clung to each other until their shudders slowed and finally stopped.

Merry didn't know how long they stayed in each other's arms without moving. She just knew this was a perfect moment in time and moving would mean it was over.

As if suddenly coming to his senses, Hunter rolled to the side. "Oh, God, I'm crushing you."

"No—"

But he slid away and off the bed. Seconds later a light in the bathroom went on. She missed the warmth of his body, his arms around her. And as quickly as that thought formed, he was back. He lifted the covers and slid in beside her, drawing her against his chest.

She stretched her arm over his abdomen and snuggled close. "I'm speechless."

"I don't believe that." There was laughter in his voice.

"It's true. I'm sleepy, but most of all very happy."

Silence stretched between them longer

than it should have. He didn't move a muscle but his tension was obvious. "Merry, we need to talk."

Those were words no one ever wanted to hear, especially after sex. "Okay. What's on your mind?"

"I'm thinking that we should keep this... change in status to ourselves."

"I see." She tried to keep her tone light in spite of the jab that statement gave to her heart. "Although you should know I wasn't planning to broadcast this on social media."

"I didn't mean that." He brushed his thumb over her shoulder. "It's just that our arrangement is delicate and I don't want any fallout for you."

"I appreciate that." He was being noble again. She tried to read his expression but his face was in shadow. "We're not doing anything wrong, Hunter. We established that downstairs, before—"

"I know. It's just..." He sighed. "If anyone figures out our relationship has changed, there's no way Wren won't find out. I don't know about you, but I wouldn't look forward to *those* questions."

She realized that was a joke. He was trying to ease the tension and she appreciated that. And, of course, he was right. His child was their number one consideration. "I agree that Wren should be protected."

"I knew you'd understand."

She understood what he was saying but sensed there was more he wasn't. He wanted to keep the two of them a secret and she would bet anything that it wasn't all about his daughter. He was holding something back and she couldn't shake the feeling that it had something to do with protecting himself.

A few days after the best night Hunter could remember in a very long time, he kept his promise to help Merry move. At her house, he and Wilder picked up a recliner and carried it to the enclosed rental truck backed into the driveway. They tucked it snugly between a full-size mattress and the small dinette set.

"This is the last thing going in here." Hunter's cell phone pinged and he glanced at the text message. "It's from Wren."

"Is she okay?" Wilder asked.

He looked at it. "Yeah. She and Gramps are decorating his tree."

"I know she wanted to help Merry move. How did you get her to stay at the Ambling A?"

"I didn't." Hunter smiled at the memory. "Somehow Merry convinced her that she was helping with the move more than anyone by keeping Gramps company."

His brother lifted his Stetson and then set it more firmly on his head. "She sure has a way with your daughter."

Not just Wren. Hunter couldn't forget holding Merry in his arms and making love to her. And the questions shadowing her eyes when he'd asked her to keep their secret. The last thing he wanted was for his brother to know.

"There are still some boxes in the kitchen and garage," Hunter said. "Why don't you go on ahead and drive this load to the storage unit. Everything that's left will fit in her truck and mine."

"Here she comes now."

Hunter saw that Merry was carrying a square, clear glass platter. And she looked very close to tears.

"Can we put this in the truck?" she asked. "I found it when you guys moved the hutch in the kitchen."

"What is it?" Hunter asked.

"My mother's serving tray. It has her initials etched in the glass—IMM—Ina May Matthews. Dad gave it to her on her last birthday and she loved it." She was talking a lot, a sure sign that she was trying too hard to be in good spirits. "It's an awkward size, though, and didn't fit in the cupboards so Dad stood it up behind the hutch. I'd forgotten all about it until today."

Hunter could see the emotional strain in the dark circles beneath her eyes and the tightness in her mouth. He took it from her. "Sure, we've got room for that. But I think if you've got some towels handy, or sheets, we should wrap it up. Keep it from getting chipped or scratched."

She nodded and brushed a hand across her cheek. "There are some towels in that box in the garage."

After she walked away Wilder shook his head. "This has to be really tough on her. Moving out so soon after losing her dad. In a couple of months her whole life has changed."

"Yeah."

Hunter knew the changes had started when her father was diagnosed with cancer. There were appointments for treatment and eventually she gave up college classes and a boyfriend to take care of him. And finally planning a funeral and selling the house. He had no idea how she stayed so darn positive and cheerful through it all and admired the hell out of her because she managed to.

She came back with a couple of blue bath

towels and a roll of duct tape, then took the tray and wrapped it up securely. After climbing up into the rear of the truck, she wedged the bundle between the mattress and box spring.

Smiling sadly, she said, "Mom and Dad are together again."

"That's a nice way of looking at it," Hunter said.

"I think so." She pressed her full lips together, probably to keep the grief from spilling out.

Hunter wished there was something he could do or say to make her feel better but he came up empty. In the end he reached out and put his hands at her waist, lifting her down. If Wilder hadn't been there, he'd have pulled her into his arms and just held her. But he couldn't, since he was the one who'd insisted they keep the personal turn in their relationship a secret.

Wilder cleared his throat. "So, Merry, Hunter suggested I drive this stuff over to your storage unit while he helps you put everything else in the pickup trucks. Then you can meet me there."

She looked concerned. "But we're going to be a little while. You can't unload this truck by yourself."

He shrugged. "I'm going to grab something to eat and I'll make some SOS calls. Logan. Knox. Xander. Finn. One or all of them will give me a hand."

"I've already inconvenienced one third of the Crawford brothers. I feel bad asking for more help."

"You're not asking. I am," Wilder insisted. "Although I will drop your name because they'll do it for you, not me. They like you."

"If you're sure…" She looked hesitant but he waved a hand in dismissal of her concerns. "I don't know how to thank you. Both of you."

She met Hunter's gaze and he knew he would do anything for her if she kept looking at him that way. The powerful feeling rocked him to the core.

"Don't mention it." Wilder looked at him

and held out his hand. "Do you have the keys to the truck?"

"Yeah." Hunter had picked up the rental and driven it here. He fished the keys out of his jeans pocket and handed them over. Then the two of them pulled down and latched the truck's rear sliding door. "When we're finished here, we'll meet you there."

Wilder hesitated a second, then gave Merry a quick hug. "We got this, Mer."

"It's really sweet of you to help. Thanks again."

The smile she gifted his brother with actually made Hunter jealous. He knew Wilder was just being neighborly, supportive, but for reasons he didn't want to explore that didn't seem to matter. Some primal part of him turned green with jealousy at the thought of any man touching her. Even his brother, who he knew was just being a friend. What the hell was wrong with him?

These thoughts scrolled through his mind as he and Merry stood in the driveway and watched the truck slowly rumble away down the street. Almost everything she had in the world was going into storage. It was like stepping into limbo. He had experienced that feeling in Texas when he'd packed up for the move to Rust Creek Falls. But for him it was a fresh start.

Life as Merry knew it was ending. Her second job with him helped make ends meet. That and the roof over her head were dependent on him. He felt the crushing weight of that responsibility, especially because he'd crossed a line and slept with her. Every night since had been a test of his willpower not to have her again. He resisted the temptation because it had been more than physical and he didn't want to get in deeper emotionally. And the thought went through his mind one more time: What the hell was wrong with him?

"I'm going to back my truck into the driveway." Merry was looking up at him.

"Hmm?" He forced his thoughts back to her.

"To load boxes."

"Right. I'll do it for you." He held out his hand for the keys and she dropped them into his palm.

"Thanks. I've got cartons scattered in different rooms. I'll move them all to the garage."

"Okay."

Hunter moved the truck, then began to load up the rear bed while Merry brought out the rest of the things from the house. One by one she carried cartons to the tailgate and let him arrange them, maximizing space. More than once he saw her lift out a book, or a framed picture and stare sadly before replacing it and folding the flaps of the box. Every time, he could swear that it was like a sharp stab in her heart. And every time, he wanted to take her in his arms and tell her it was going to be fine.

She lifted a box up to him. "This is the last one."

He took it and rearranged some cartons, nodding in satisfaction when he finished.

"It's all snug in there. Nothing is going to slide around."

"Good. The Realtor is setting up a cleaning before the new owners move in so I guess this is it." She looked up. "I'm going to walk through and make sure I didn't miss anything."

"Okay." He watched her go into the garage and disappear through the door and into the house.

She looked fragile and heartbreakingly alone and his instincts were urging him to comfort her somehow. He understood the heartbreak of losing a loved one. Part of him wanted to keep his distance. He didn't want to care about her, not deeply. But he cared enough and just couldn't stand back and let her face this final goodbye all by herself.

Hunter found her standing in the center of the empty living room staring at the corner. "Merry."

She jumped. "I didn't hear you come in."

"I just wanted to check up on you. Everything okay?"

"Yes." There wasn't much conviction in her voice though. "No. Not really."

"What are you looking at?"

She released a shuddering breath. "That's where we put the Christmas tree. I was just remembering the holidays we had in this house."

He moved beside her and slid his arm across her shoulders because words alone wouldn't ease her sorrow. "It's a crappy time to have to move."

"Any time would be hard." She leaned into him. "I know it's just a house. But—"

"What?"

"I feel as if I'm losing him again."

"I understand." He was pretty sure he did. "When I left the house in Texas where I lived with Lara, I felt something like you're feeling now. But it wasn't all bad. It was time for a change of scene."

"I know you're trying to help," she said. "And I appreciate it very much. But I just feel so lost."

Hunter studied her face and saw how hard

she was trying to be brave and not give in to the profound grief, and his heart squeezed painfully. He would never be sure whether it was for her or himself, but he folded her against him.

"It's okay, Merry. Feel the feelings."

Her shoulders shook with sobs then and he held her, doing his damnedest not to take his own advice and feel his own feelings. He badly wanted to tell her that he would make it okay. But he knew better than anyone that was impossible. And if he gave in to this urge to try and fix her heartache, he would be risking a pain he was all too familiar with. Losing someone a second time would destroy him. And not only him. Wren was already attached to Merry. He didn't want to deepen the bond by crossing a line and hurt his daughter, too.

Everything inside of him was saying, *Don't care for this woman.* And he was trying his damnedest not to. But somehow Merry was invading his heart in spite of his resolve. And he didn't know how to make it stop.

Chapter Thirteen

"You are going to be a fantastic reindeer." The play was going to start soon and Hunter was backstage trying to reassure his anxious child. That was a tall order since he looked a little frantic himself.

"I'm scared, Daddy."

Merry recognized the classic signs of stage fright because she'd experienced it herself.

After countless hours memorizing lines and practicing being Rudolph's best reindeer friend, Wren knew her part backward and forward. In fact, preparation had consumed them in the days after Merry had moved out of her house. She was grateful for the distraction because it had kept her from dwelling on the sadness of saying goodbye. And she was thankful that Hunter had held her when she cried. It was the last time he'd touched her and she'd been waiting for a good time to talk to him about that. But first the play. One crisis at a time.

Spectators and performers were gathering in the Rust Creek Falls Community Center. It was bigger than the school's multipurpose room in order to accommodate the students and their families, along with anyone else in town who wanted to attend. Most people did. Wren's whole family, headed by her beloved Gramps, were all out in the audience somewhere.

The noise level was high, which probably added to the anxiety. Wren was already in her one-piece reindeer costume. Merry had pulled the child's blond hair up onto the crown of her head, then curled the long strands and made ringlets. She'd used brown eyebrow pencil to darken her little nose and there was only one accessory left.

"Let's put this on." Merry was holding a brown headband with antlers attached. After the little girl's tentative nod, she slid it into place then fluffed out the curls. "Oh, my—"

"What? Is it bad?" Wren asked anxiously.

Hunter took a picture with his cell phone. "You look great."

"It's kind of like a tiara," Merry said.

"Can a reindeer be a princess?" she asked.

"Yes," Hunter said instantly. "As far as I'm concerned you are Dancer, the reindeer princess. Reindeer are the only deer species in which the females also grow antlers. So, tap into your inner royalty and you'll do fine."

"I'm afraid I might forget my lines."

If possible, Hunter looked even more nervous than his daughter. "I don't suppose it would help to tell her to picture the audience in their underwear," he whispered to Merry.

She shook her head. "She's probably too young to understand the concept."

"I'm a parent. I feel like I should know just

what to say that would help her not freeze up." Frustration darkened his eyes.

Merry had thought a lot about her parents since cleaning out the house. She'd gone through a lot of mementos she kept of her mother and a memory came back to her now, as clearly as if it had happened yesterday.

She went down on one knee in front of the little girl. "When I was about your age I was in a school play, too. I was so frightened I could hardly talk. But my mother said something to me that really helped."

"What?"

"She said, 'When you come out on stage, just look for me in the audience. And remember that I love you, no matter what.'"

"Okay." The little girl nodded.

Merry gave her a hug, then stood. "So if you're nervous, look for me."

Hunter was standing next to a break in the curtains and peeked out. He moved next to her and whispered in her ear. "It's starting to fill up out there. Why don't you go grab a couple of seats before all the good ones are gone. I'll stay here with Wren."

His breath stirred the hair by her ear and made her shiver with awareness. Part of her wanted to melt into him. The other part that was annoyingly rational knew that was a bad idea.

"Okay." She looked at Wren. "We are going to be right where you can see us. Break a leg. That's a show business expression that means you're going to do great."

Merry gave her one last reassuring smile, then exited stage right and surveyed the audience seating, concentrating on the center seats near the front. She spotted two in the second row and moved quickly to grab the chairs.

There was an older woman sitting next to them and Merry made eye contact. She indicated the two empty chairs. "Are these taken?"

"They are now." The silver-haired woman smiled. She looked to be somewhere in her sixties.

Merry sat beside her and plopped her purse on the empty chair to make sure it was saved for Hunter. "Thanks."

"I've seen you around town but I don't believe we've met. I'm Linda Dempsey."

"Merry Matthews. I'm an educational aide at the elementary school."

"Your father is Ed, right? The electrician? I heard he passed away a few months ago. I'm very sorry for your loss."

"Thank you."

The woman's expression was sincerely sympathetic. "Your dad did good work. And he was a nice man. He'll be missed by folks in this town."

"That's very nice of you to say." It was comforting to know the father she'd loved so much would be fondly remembered. "How long have you lived in Rust Creek Falls?"

"All my life. Born and raised here." She smiled wickedly and her expression was decidedly conspiratorial when she leaned closer. "I know I don't look old enough, but I've seen my share of feuds, clandestine affairs and generally outrageous behavior involving some or most of this town's prominent families. Not much stays secret around here. Rust Creek Falls isn't that big and gossip spreads fast."

"Sounds like some interesting history," Merry commented.

"That's for sure." Linda glanced at the stage where the sound of young voices drifted from behind the curtain. "Do you have a child in the play tonight?"

"Yes. No. Well, kind of." She laughed and shrugged. "In addition to my other job I'm also a nanny for Hunter Crawford's little girl."

"So that's you. I heard he hired someone." The older woman looked thoughtful. "Didn't the Crawfords buy the Ambling A Ranch? The old Abernathy place?"

"Yes." She remembered the diary discovered beneath a rotted floorboard at the main house. She'd heard the book was jewel encrusted and with the letter *A* on the front the theory was that it had belonged to one of the Abernathys. "Did you know the previous owners?"

"I heard stories about them." That didn't really answer the question.

"Stories?" There was a commotion behind her, female laughter as a group of women filled in the row.

"The Abernathys left town in the middle of the night without saying anything to anyone. The rumor was that Josiah Abernathy got a girl pregnant. And that the baby was stillborn. It's said the heartbroken mother had a breakdown and went crazy. From what I hear, it was a huge scandal at the time."

Merry heard the Crawford brothers talk about a girl being pregnant but the diary just mentioned her initial. *W.* "Do you know the pregnant woman's name?"

"No. I never heard," the woman said. "Such a sad story if it's true. I much prefer lovers to have a happy ending."

"Maybe the rumors are wrong," Merry suggested. "Maybe Josiah and his mysterious love lived happily ever after."

Linda smiled. "You're a woman after my own heart. I like you."

"Thanks. I like you, too." Merry smiled.

This woman hadn't given her much but it could be another piece of the Abernathy family puzzle. The way the Crawfords talked about the romantic passages Josiah had written to his beloved W, she had a feeling they would be very interested in this information.

She'd been so focused on what Linda was saying, Merry was surprised when she saw that the community center was nearly full. Finding two seats together was impossible now and couples were having to split up. A man she recognized as the father of a boy in Wren's class stopped at the end of her row.

He pointed to the place holding her purse. "Is that seat taken?"

She nodded. "I'm saving it for Hunter Crawford. His daughter is in the play and she's nervous so he's with her for moral support."

"Okay. Thanks anyway." He moved on.

"So, that's Hunter Crawford's nanny."

Merry heard the comment from a woman in the row behind her.

Another female voice said, "I heard they're an item."

"Well, she lives with him. That makes her awfully handy." The third comment was catty and from yet another woman.

A trio of mean girls. Merry told herself to feel sorry for them but it was hard to pull off when her face was burning with embarrassment.

Linda patted her hand. Obviously she'd overheard. "He's a very good-looking man and women notice that sort of thing. So it hasn't escaped attention that you're dating him."

This woman was right. Not much that happened in this town was missed. They'd come to the tree lighting, then had hot chocolate. People had obviously noticed, but that didn't mean they'd gotten the details right.

"We're not dating," she told Linda.

"That's probably a good thing." There was sadness and sympathy in the woman's eyes.

"It's common knowledge that he's a widower. For five years I was with a man who'd lost his wife. He never could care about me the way he did for her. In time I could see that I was never going to get my happy ending with him so I broke it off. I know from experience that competing with a dead woman for a man's heart is not just a losing proposition. It's also painful."

Merry was stunned. It had bothered her when Hunter had suggested they keep their relationship a secret. Did he not want anyone to know because he was still in love with his wife?

What if there was no room in his life for someone else? Merry knew she couldn't settle for that. Obviously he'd been hurt and could be protecting himself. She could deal with that. But there was no way to win if he was still in love with the woman he'd lost.

The day he helped her move, when he'd held her in his arms, he'd said he understood how it felt to leave a place you loved. When he left Texas he'd had to say goodbye to his wife. What if that was about still loving her?

Wren looked like she was going to cry, and walking away from her backstage was one of the hardest things Hunter had ever done. But the teacher basically kicked him out, in the politest possible way. So he gave his little girl a big smile and left.

He spotted Merry right away. Something about her thick blond curls stood out and caught his attention. Sliding past the people filling in the row, he took the seat beside her when she moved her purse.

"Thanks for saving this," he said.

"Sure."

It was only one word but something about her tone was off. He couldn't put his finger on it except that she sounded very un-Merry-like. That was to say not very cheerful.

Hunter looked at her and noticed a paleness to her normally rosy cheeks. She'd been her normal self backstage, giving Wren a pep talk.

"Are you okay?" he asked quietly.

"Fine."

The snap in her voice said otherwise. It was a reminder of how much he hated that word coming from a woman. Or maybe it was just that he knew something was bugging her and they were going to talk later. Come to think of it, he didn't like that either.

It wasn't often that circumstances saved a guy from putting his foot in his mouth, but he got lucky when the curtains parted, the house lights dimmed and a little girl was standing onstage in a red velvet dress. She was the play's narrator and set up the story of Rudolph the Red-Nosed Reindeer. There was enthusiastic applause from the standing room—only audience after her short speech. Then the eight reindeer trotted out followed by a discouraged-looking Rudolph. The big red nose was a clue to his identity.

Hunter zeroed in on Wren, who sidled up to the dejected Rudolph. He would die for his child and wanted to protect her from any conceivable hurt, including public humiliation. This was where her dialogue was supposed to start and she looked terrified, hesitating too long. His chest felt tight.

"Look at me, sweetie," Merry whispered.

Almost as if she'd heard, Wren scanned the audience and grinned. He saw that Merry was holding up her hand with the pinkie, index finger and thumb up while the other two fingers curled into her palm. The "I love you" hand sign.

His little girl turned to Rudolph and said in a loud and confident voice, "Why are you so sad?"

The words were full of emotion. She'd nailed it and he breathed a sigh of relief. The rest of the story was a traditional telling of the red-nosed reindeer dealing with teasing because he was different. After saving Santa's mission on a foggy night, he was, of course, a hero. And the last line of the presentation was Wren's.

"The moral of the story is to be kind to everyone, not just at Christmas, but every day of the year."

The small performers held hands and took a bow while the audience clapped and cheered. Hunter snapped pictures with his cell phone as did a lot of other people watching.

"She did great," he said.

"Perfect." Merry discreetly wiped away a tear. But it didn't escape his notice that she was still giving him one-word responses.

After the first graders were finished, every other elementary school class put on their performance. As each group exited the spotlight, he was aware that Merry chatted with the older woman sitting next to her but said nothing to him. He also noted that her new best friend kept giving him looks, as if sizing him up. And he caught snippets of conversation from the women in the row behind him. Enough to know that they were definitely sizing him up. Sneaking a glance, he saw that they were young and attractive.

He also experienced an odd sensation. It was weird how he felt like he was cheating on Merry by noticing the women. He wasn't married and never planned to be again. Yet she was constantly on his mind, always in his dreams, and he couldn't seem to control it. He liked everything about her. The cheerful disposition, sense of humor, positive outlook and determination to be a teacher.

On top of that, she was so damn beautiful and that hair… The way she handled Wren was nothing short of amazing. Which was why he was determined to keep things uncomplicated and not mess this up and lose her.

The overhead lights went to full brightness as the stage curtains closed, signaling the end of tonight's performances. After that, kids of all ages still wearing their costumes streamed down the aisles looking for family members and friends. Thanks to Merry, his daughter knew right where to find them.

"Hunter?"

"Hmm?" He met Merry's gaze and was surprised to see shadows in her eyes.

She indicated the woman beside her. "This is Linda. She's lived in Rust Creek Falls all her life and knows a lot about the town's history. Including the Abernathy family."

Could be she had information about the diary his brothers were so convinced was some romantic lucky charm. He didn't believe in that sort of thing.

He shook hands with the woman. "It's nice to meet you."

"Likewise. Welcome to Rust Creek Falls. Although I know you've been here a few months. Better late than never."

"Thanks."

"There's a rumor going around that your father has hired someone to introduce all his sons to women and get them married off." Her tone was teasing even as she glanced at Merry. "Heard he's been getting pretty good results with the whole thing. What with four of your brothers now spoken for."

"Dad will take any credit he can get. The truth is that he has no business peddling romance, with or without help. His own marriage was a failure because he rushed into it."

Hunter wasn't sure why he shared that information with a virtual stranger. Although he suspected it had something to do with rebelling against the thoughts he'd been having about Merry.

Linda didn't seem put off by his tone. "It's a shame about your folks. But is it a total failure when they have six strapping sons to show for it?"

And his mother walked out on all of them. That abandonment was and always would be a part of him. And all it meant was that his parents had sex at least six times but that didn't mean they were happy.

"From what I hear, your married brothers are head over heels in love," the woman said.

He wanted to say they were for now, but that made him sound like the Grinch. He couldn't help it. Every time he thought about Avery's pregnancy and the things that could go wrong, it bothered him. And the fact that all of his brothers were talking about starting families meant more worry. From his perspective, it was hard not to look at the dark side.

Maybe a subject change was in order. "How is it you're here for the play? Do you have grandchildren at the school?"

"No. I never married."

"I see." Merry sighed a bit sadly.

"I can see you're feeling sorry for me. Don't. I'm resigned to it now. And the way I see it, all the elementary school kids are mine. I come every year to support them. They're so doggone cute. And that little one of yours is a real sweetheart," she said to Hunter.

"You'll get no argument from me." He grinned. Looking around, he noticed that the place was emptying out pretty fast. "Speaking of Wren, I wonder where she is. Maybe I should go look for her."

Linda stood. "It's time to take my old self home. Nice to meet you, Merry. And you, too, Hunter. Happy holidays."

"Same to you," they both said.

"Now go find that little angel of yours. Or

should I say *reindeer*." She grinned. "Good night."

Linda left the row and Hunter was alone with Merry. She wouldn't look at him and he was about to ask her what was going on. But just then he spotted his daughter skipping toward them with a happy smile on her face. She headed over to their row, squeezed right past him and threw herself into Merry's arms.

"I saw you and then I remembered my lines. This is the best day ever," she said.

"You were fantastic, kiddo," Hunter told her. "You got all your lines and it was an awesome performance. There's never been a better one in the history of school plays."

"No, Daddy." She climbed into Merry's lap and snuggled close for a moment.

"No, what? I think you did a great job."

"That's not why it's the best day." She smiled tenderly up at her nanny. "It's the best because I finally had a dad and a mom to see me. Just like all the other kids."

He felt as if he'd been sucker punched.

When Wren's mom died, he'd always been thankful that she was too young to remember and feel the agonizing pain of losing her. Now he knew she felt it anyway. How could he not have seen how much she missed having a mother? How much she wanted one.

He'd been afraid of her getting too attached to Merry, but here they were. She'd stepped seamlessly into the role of mom, and his daughter had responded to that with love.

He should have realized there was no way to shield her. When he hired Merry he was damned either way.

And what about him? Just a little while ago he'd been thinking he liked everything about Merry. And he couldn't get her out of his mind. Was he starting to love her, too? After so short a time?

That would be rushing into a relationship just like his father had done. A disaster scenario with history repeating itself. Even if he believed it would be different for him, he'd loved a woman once and losing her nearly destroyed him. Raising Wren had forced him to put one foot in front of the other. But if he let someone in and lost her again, it wasn't just about him. This time he would have to watch his daughter be destroyed, too. He couldn't stand that. He wouldn't do it.

Abruptly he stood. "It's getting late. We need to get home."

Chapter Fourteen

Wren chattered happily on the drive back to the ranch. Merry wished Hunter would say something but he didn't, not much anyway. This awkward silence was about his daughter saying that she was like all the other kids with a dad and a *mom*.

When that child had enthusiastically climbed into her lap, Merry's heart had never felt so full. She loved the little girl so much and apparently Wren returned the feelings. Why would he have a problem with someone loving his little girl? Love was good, right?

And Merry had never consciously tried to take her mother's place.

Suddenly she knew what the problem was and felt cold all the way to her soul. It was about love, all right, but not hers for Wren. This had to do with Wren's mother.

To finally meet a man who could love so deeply and completely was nothing short of astonishing. And clearly the universe was having a great laugh at Merry's expense. Why else would she realize that she was in love with him and figure out at the same time that he'd never stopped loving the woman he'd lost?

"Daddy, can I stay up a little later tonight? I don't have school tomorrow."

"You don't have school for the next couple of weeks. The play just kicked off your holiday vacation." Hunter had just turned onto the road leading to the Ambling A. In the distance, lights from the compound of buildings were visible through the darkness. "What do you think about her staying up later?"

The question snapped Merry out of her dark place. She tried to make her response as lighthearted and normal as possible. "Well, since you don't have to get up early, I think the success of your theater debut should be celebrated."

"Can we do that with hot chocolate and cookies?" the little girl asked.

Merry would prefer something a little stronger to take the edge off the ache in her heart, but this was all about Wren. "That sounds like the perfect thing."

She stole a glance at Hunter, who was nailing the role of the strong, silent type. The sharp angles of his profile were outlined by the truck's dashboard lights and the intensity surrounding him was sucking all the oxygen from the air. At least for her. These weeks with him and his daughter had been some of the best in her life but now everything was awful. Wren was a bright little girl and would notice the tension. She noticed everything.

Hunter pulled up to the house and turned

off the truck, then they all got out. Just as he was opening the front door of the log cabin, her cell phone rang. She looked at the caller ID and saw that it was her brother, Jack. Things were tense between them, too, but talking to him would be a welcome break from Hunter's exhausting silence.

She answered and said, "Hi, Jack."

"Hey, Merry. How are things?"

A little while ago things took a turn into suckiness, but thank you for asking, she thought.

"Hold on for a second, Jack." She put her hand over the phone and said, "It's my brother."

"Okay. Wren and I will go whip up some hot chocolate and give you privacy."

After he hustled his daughter into the kitchen, she stepped into the living room and stood beside the Christmas tree in the front window. It was the farthest she could get from the kitchen. Not that she was going to say anything personal about Hunter, but... Better safe than sorry. How ironic was that thought? She knew a lot about sorry but had very little experience with safe.

She put the phone to her ear again. "How are you, Jack?"

"Fine."

"Good." But it didn't sound like he was fine. Still, how would she know? They'd barely spent any time together since she was a little girl who'd lost her mother.

"How are you?" he asked.

Shouldn't be a problem pulling off a lie. Once they'd been close, but he couldn't read her like a book anymore. "I'm fine."

"You don't sound fine," he said.

Well, color her surprised. "Okay. You don't sound fine either."

He laughed. "I'm as fine as can be expected what with being halfway around the world at the holidays."

"Can you tell me where you are? Or would you have to kill me?" She smiled at the memory of his very first deployment when he'd started that joke.

"Where I am doesn't matter." No question about it. He wasn't fine either.

"Are you in danger?" Her chest went tight at the thought of something happening to him. The two of them had their problems but the idea of him not being on this earth at all was inconceivable to her. She loved him and he was all the family she had left.

"That's not why I'm calling." The non-answer was probably a yes on the danger thing. "I'm coming home for Christmas."

"That's great." And it was, but things had changed dramatically since his whirlwind visit for their dad's memorial service.

"But?"

"How do you know there's a but?" she said.

"I know you. I could hear it in your voice."

She let out a long breath. "Jack, I was Dad's executor and he left the house to me because you were gone, and I wasn't."

"Okay."

"I had to sell it. I couldn't pay the mortgage without the income from Dad's business. And without him there was no business."

"Why didn't you tell me?" He sounded shocked and upset.

This was not the time to get into all that. When they were face-to-face, they could discuss why she did what she did. "It was the best option. I'll tell you when I see you."

"Okay. But what about you? Where are you living?" There was a protective note in his voice that brought back flashes of their once-cherished relationship.

"I've taken a live-in nanny job. I'm okay."

Was telling a lie so close to Christmas worse than a lie any other time of the year? Probably. But being on Santa's naughty list would save the big guy a trip, for her anyway.

"Okay, then," he said.

"I'm sorry, Jack. If I'd known you were coming, I'd have put off the sale. But I didn't. And I can't ask my boss to put you up." Unexpected disappointment rocked her. She hadn't realized just how much she needed to see her brother. For so long she'd felt alone, but something about hearing his voice tapped into a deep well of yearning for the bond they'd once shared.

"Don't worry, sis. I'll be there before Christmas and figure something out."

"Okay. I can't wait to see you." That was truer now than ever before.

"Gotta go. Bye, Mer."

"Travel safe and—" The line went dead. Loneliness like she'd never known settled heavily on her heart.

She shook it off as best she could because she had a job to do. For the moment anyway.

She walked into the kitchen and tried to act as if nothing was wrong. Wren was sitting at the table with a mug of hot chocolate in front of her and beside it a small plate with a reindeer cookie on it.

"So, how goes the celebration?"

The little girl shrugged. "Okay. Daddy's hot chocolate isn't as good as yours."

A small victory but Merry would take it. She met Hunter's gaze for the first time since his daughter had said what she had at the community center and changed everything between them. His eyes were dark and guarded.

"Sorry about that," she said, holding up her phone. "I haven't talked to Jack in a while."

"How is he?" The tone was polite but cool.

"Fine." So he'd said. "He's coming for Christmas."

Almost too quickly Hunter said, "I'm sure you're looking forward to spending as much time with him as possible. Why don't you take the week off, with pay, and have a quality visit?"

"But, Daddy, it's our first Christmas in Rust Creek Falls." The little girl's eyes suddenly filled with tears. "It won't be the best one ever if Merry isn't here."

"Oh, hell," Hunter mumbled. Then he went down on one knee beside her chair. "But, kiddo, her brother has been gone a long time. They have a lot of catching up to do."

Obviously he wanted her anywhere but here and that made Merry's heart hurt more than she'd have thought possible. "Sweetie, don't cry. You'll have a wonderful holiday with your dad and Gramps and your aunts and uncles and cousin."

As big fat tears rolled down her cheeks, Wren turned her tragic gaze on first her father then Merry. "It won't be wonderful. Why can't your brother stay here with us for Christmas? We have room. Right, Daddy?"

"We do." Hunter was crumbling under the weight of her sad expression. "Of course he can stay. But that's up to Merry and her brother."

Now it was her turn to feel the full force of not being able to tell this little girl no. It was also an answer to the problem of where Jack could stay on such short notice. She looked at Hunter. "If you're sure? I promise he won't be any trouble. We'll do our own thing—"

"He's more than welcome. Giving a soldier serving his country a place to spend Christmas is the very least we can do."

The words were right but it felt all wrong. A few hours earlier this would have made everything perfect but not now. "Thank you, Hunter. I'll let Jack know."

Wren hugged her father. "It's going to be the best Christmas ever."

"Whatever you say. But now I think it's time for bed."

"Okay."

Without another word to him Merry took the little girl upstairs for a quick bath and bedtime story before lights out. She remembered all the fun and carefree nights since she'd come to work for Hunter. Especially that night in his bed, in his arms. Now she knew there wouldn't be any more sweet and happy times in this house.

More than anything Merry wanted to go to her room and curl up on her bed, but there was something she had to do first. She went downstairs and found Hunter in the living room staring at the Christmas tree. He was holding a glass with a small amount of Scotch in it.

"Can I talk to you?" she asked.

"Of course." He downed the rest of the liquid in his glass then turned To look at her. "Is Wren okay?"

Merry couldn't help a small smile. "Zonked. It's exhausting being a star."

"Yeah. The meltdown was a clue."

"About that…" She stuffed her hands into her jeans pockets to hide the fact they were shaking. "It's really not necessary for you to put Jack up while he's on leave. We can make other arrangements."

He shook his head. "I meant what I said. He's a soldier and it would be my honor to have him here. Show my gratitude for the sacrifices he's made for his country. And my daughter wants you here."

"Okay. But there's something I have to tell you and that might change your mind."

He frowned and his gaze never left her face. "What?"

"I'm giving my two weeks' notice."

"You're quitting?"

"Yes."

"But I thought you liked it here."

More than she could possibly put into words. But that was before. Now she knew he couldn't return her feelings and it was just too hard. And there was no way she could tell him that.

"Your daughter is—" Emotion closed off her throat so she simply put her hand over her heart to express her deep feelings for his child. "But you and I both know this arrangement was only temporary. So it's best to make a clean break. I won't abandon her at Christmas or leave you in the lurch while she's out of school. But I'm going to start the new year with an aggressive push to finish classes and get my teaching credentials."

"I see."

Merry blinked at him. She wasn't sure what she'd wanted to hear, but that wasn't it. Something along the lines of begging her to stay would have been nice. And that's when she realized hope was hands down the cruelest of all emotions. It set you up just to disappoint you again. And the second time was so much more painful and disheartening.

The chance to get out of this encounter with her dignity intact was slowly slipping away. It took the last reserves of her strength to smile but she managed a shaky one.

"I just wanted to let you know so you could start looking for someone else to be Wren's nanny." That said, she left the room and went up the stairs before hope could blindside her again.

Mostly she had to get away before her façade crumbled and Hunter could see that she was in love with him. Tomorrow she would worry about how she was going to hide that truth and pretend nothing had changed. For the record, this was going to be her worst Christmas ever.

On Christmas Eve, Merry was alone in the cabin, waiting for her brother to arrive. Hunter had taken Wren to the big house for dinner with his father and brother. It would give his little girl a chance to work off some Christmas anticipation energy. Max and Wilder could help with that.

Merry had been invited but declined to go, wanting to be here when Jack showed up.

Hunter had seemed relieved but Wren didn't censor her disappointment. It hurt Merry's heart because in a very short time she would not be the child's nanny. But she was trying not to think about that. In a few hours it would be Christmas and Jack had said he would be here. But why should his visit go the way she wanted? The rest of her life certainly wasn't.

That's the Christmas spirit, she told herself. A pity party during the most wonderful time of the year. Bah humbug!

She started pacing and kept checking her phone for messages, but there was nothing. Maybe nothing was all she could ever expect from Jack Matthews. But he'd sounded lonely. And sad. And very sure he'd be here in time for Christmas. How would she even know who to call to find him? What if—

A knock on the door kept her from going to a very dark place and she rushed to answer it. There on the porch was a man dressed in military camouflage and a matching fleece-lined jacket.

"Jack!" Merry threw herself into his arms, forgetting their differences in the sheer joy and relief that her big brother was safe, and more importantly, here. "I was getting worried."

"Traveling with the military is not an exact science." He hugged her tight, then held her at arm's length. "It's so good to see you, Merry. You're beautiful."

"You, too. Not beautiful. Just good to see you." She laughed and opened the door wider. "Come in. How did you get here? I'd have picked you up in—well, wherever you were."

He walked inside and looked around. "I caught a ride from a buddy who lives in Kalispell."

She looked at the duffel in his hand. "I'll show you where your room is so you can stow that."

"Okay." He followed her up the stairs and into the empty room next to hers.

"Hunter managed to find a mattress and box spring in storage up at the big house. I hope it's comfortable. You'll have to share the bathroom with me and Wren—"

"The little girl you take care of?"

"Yes. I can't wait for you to meet her. You're going to love her."

"And the father? Am I going to love him, too?"

Merry hadn't seen that protective look in his eyes for a long time. "Hunter is a good man and a devoted father." And that's all she was going to say about that. "Are you hungry? I'll fix us something to eat."

"It's past dinnertime. You haven't eaten yet?"

"I couldn't. I was worried about you," she said.

"Yeah, I could eat." Dark circles under his eyes were a clue that he was exhausted as well as hungry.

"It's just leftover stew," she warned, "but Hunter said it was the best he'd ever tasted."

She chattered away as they walked downstairs and kept it up while she reheated the food. Before long they were sitting at the table, eating. Jack scarfed his dinner up in record time.

"How about a second helping?" she asked. "Before you answer, you should know there are fresh baked cookies, too. Mom's recipe."

The sparkle in his blue eyes dimmed. "I don't think I could eat another bite. But thanks, Mer."

It didn't escape her notice that his expression changed at the mention of their mother. But before she could call him on it, the front door opened and closed. Moments later Wren ran into the kitchen and came to a screeching halt when she saw the new arrival. Hunter was right behind her.

"Are you Jack?" the little girl asked.

"I am."

"My name is Wren. You're finally here. Merry was waitin' a long time. It took you forever, Jack."

"He's Mr. Matthews," Hunter corrected her.

"Jack is fine with me if that's okay with

you." He stood up and held out his hand to Hunter. "Nice to meet you."

"Same here. Hunter Crawford," he said, gripping the other man's hand.

Merry watched them sizing each other up. Both were big men, muscular and solidly built. Jack's hair was lighter, a dirty blond, and would have riotous curls like hers if allowed to grow longer than his short military cut. The two of them reminded her of predators circling each other, waiting for a show of weakness.

Jack broke the standoff. "I want to thank you for your hospitality. I'm sorry it was last minute but I appreciate you letting me stay here for Christmas."

"Happy to have you. Thank you for your service," Hunter said.

Wren looked way up at her brother. "Santa's comin' tonight, Jack."

He hunkered down to her level. "That's right. Have you been naughty or nice this year?"

"Mostly nice," she answered. "And Daddy says that Santa knows no one is perfect."

Jack laughed and Merry realized she hadn't seen that in a very long time. The magic of a child to touch someone's heart in a miraculous way was beyond measure.

"How was your dinner?" Merry asked her.

"Fun. Gramps let me open one of my presents. It's a princess Christmas nightgown."

"I can't wait to see it on you." Technically Merry had seen it. Max had requested her assistance for ideas and she'd bought it. "She loves princesses." That was for Jack's benefit.

"Can I get ready for bed now?" Wren was practically quivering with excitement.

"I think that can be arranged," her father said. "I'll supervise so Merry can visit with her brother."

"Yay!" Wren clapped her hands together then said to Jack, "I'll see you later."

"I look forward to that."

She ran out of the room and Hunter started to follow. He stopped in the doorway then turned and said to Merry, "Mission accomplished."

"You're welcome."

When they were gone Jack asked, "What was that all about?"

"Her grandfather asked me for gift ideas and I suggested the nightgown, knowing she would want to put it on right away. So it checked two boxes—a gift to open Christmas Eve and an incentive to get ready for bed and, if a miracle happens, go to sleep at a reasonable hour." She shrugged. "It worked."

"That's something Mom would have done," Jack said wistfully.

She'd been young when their mom died and wouldn't have recognized this as one of her strategic moves. Not without her brother to point it out. "Really?"

"Yeah. You remind me a lot of her."

"I remember her saying you were her first-born, the one she spent the most time with. You loved her a lot, didn't you?" She put a plate of cookies on the table, then poured him a glass of cold milk.

"Yes." Sadness welled in his eyes. "I know you did, too."

"I was devastated. And Dad was drowning in grief when she died. Then you joined the military and went away." She met his gaze and didn't bother to even try and hide the hurt and resentment in her own. "It felt as if I lost my whole family. As if I was alone. The big brother I adored, the one I looked up to, the one who was my hero and always protected me, was just gone. You abandoned me, Jack."

He stared at her for several moments as if he was lining up his argument, then just sighed. "I'm so sorry, Mer."

"Why did you disappear? How could you do that to me? To Dad?"

"Mom was sick for a long time." He took one of the cookies and broke off a piece but didn't eat it. "She got sicker, thinner. She died a little more every day. Pieces of me died along with her. After she was gone I just had to get out of there, away from all the painful memories."

"I guess I was one of them." Merry couldn't hold back anymore. It didn't matter that tomorrow was Christmas. This conversation was long overdue. It would either make things better between them, or he'd never speak to her again. Either way she had to get rid of the bitterness that was eating away at her. "Because you got away from me, too, and Dad."

"Not my finest hour."

"I took care of Dad alone, Jack. There was no one to share the pain and burden. You were his son and you couldn't even get home to see him."

"Yeah." He crushed the cookie into crumbs. "I was on a military mission, but that's not an excuse. I should have tried harder to be there for both of you."

"Damn right. You were in and out of his memorial service so fast it made my head spin."

"I know. You have every right to be angry."

"I don't need your permission. It sucked and I'm still pretty mad at you."

"I deserve that. All I can say is losing Mom just broke me. I was stupid, impulsive. Young."

"Not as young as me," she snapped.

He pushed the plate away. "If it's any consolation, I've been paying a big price for what I did. I loved her so much and it feels as if I've been running from love ever since."

He looked so completely miserable that Merry didn't have the heart to keep this up. The anger she'd carried around for so long seemed to explode inside her and then the fragments just went poof and disappeared. Gone.

She put her hand on his arm. "I understand."

"How can you? You were just a little girl."

"Losing Mom is a part of me, of who I am. A motherless little girl." She met his gaze. "Wren never knew her mother. She died from complications of childbirth."

"Damn." Jack looked shocked.

"The Crawfords moved from Texas and when she started school here, I sensed something, the void in her life, and responded to it. I'm grown up now and I get it. I understand how it feels to grow up without a mom. It's one of the reasons I took the job as her nanny. And it's why I'm still here through the holidays even though all I want is—"

"What?" Jack prompted. "To leave?"

"I didn't say that." But she'd said way more than she meant to. "It's just been hard losing Dad. Selling the house. My life isn't what I planned but I'm making it work. I refuse to settle. I'm—"

"In love with Hunter," Jack finished for her.

"Why in the world would you jump to that conclusion?"

"I saw the way you looked at him."

"Oh, please," she scoffed. "You're a guy."

"I am a guy, but I'm also your brother. I know you. Just because I've been an idiot doesn't mean that the bond we shared is gone. I can read you like a schematic. You're in love with Hunter Crawford."

She winced. "A little louder and they can hear you in downtown Rust Creek Falls."

"You haven't said I'm wrong," he pointed out.

She met his gaze and realized taking responsibility for your actions and feelings worked both ways. He'd been honest about what he'd done and why. The least she could do was be truthful about her own situation.

"Okay. As much as it pains me to say this, you're right. I am in love with him."

"But you're going to walk away?"

"I have no choice. When Wren goes back to school after New Year's, I will no longer be her nanny. I have to go. It's too hard to be around him when he's still in love with the wife he lost."

"So you've talked to him about this?"

"Well, no. I just gave him my notice, but—"

"No. Mer—" Jack put his hand over hers. "Running away because you're afraid isn't the answer. Trust me. I know all about that. I've been doing it for a long time."

"So you're saying I should fight for him?"

"Only you can decide whether or not he's worth fighting for. If he is..." Jack shrugged. "You'll know what to do."

In spite of her doubts and fears, Merry smiled. "It's so good to have you back. You're still my hero, Jack."

"I'm glad." His eyes twinkled for a moment then he turned serious. "But something tells me I might need to make room for someone else on this pedestal."

Chapter Fifteen

Merry was alone after Jack went to bed. It felt so wonderful clearing the air with him, and she filed their repaired relationship under Christmas miracles. But she was restless after their talk and ended up in the front room, sitting on the floor by the lighted Christmas tree with brightly wrapped packages underneath. She couldn't help thinking about what he'd said. Would it be more painful to tell Hunter about her feelings and drive him away? Or to lose him without ever having tried?

Before he went upstairs, she and Jack had reminisced about past Christmas Eves when she was little. Their father had made a big deal out of leaving milk and cookies out for Santa Claus, but there was always a carrot for the reindeer, too. The memory made her smile. Death couldn't steal everything from her, but it also made her miss her dad more than ever.

He had an opinion on every boy she ever liked and she used to roll her eyes at him, especially when the review was negative. But he'd always been right. What would he think of Hunter Crawford? Would he advise her not to give up without a fight? What she wouldn't give to have him here, be able to talk to him one more time.

Lights from the tree reflected in the window but she caught a glimpse of fat white flakes floating past. It was starting to snow. She smiled, remembering Wren telling her about mistlesnow wishes. Heck, what could it hurt?

She rolled to her feet and looked outside.

"Daddy, if you can hear me, I wish you would give me a sign. I'm leaning toward fighting for him, but it would sure help to know what you think."

"Merry?" It was Hunter. "Are you okay?"

She thought she was alone and his voice startled her. Taking a deep breath, she turned to face him. "I suppose that depends on whether or not you think it's okay to talk to yourself."

"In my experience you always have something smart to say, so…" He shrugged.

That was something anyway. "You're still up."

"Yeah, it took Wren a while to settle down. I guess your brother called it a night?"

"He did. Traveling for over twenty-four hours is exhausting. I insisted he get some rest. He finally gave in when he kept falling asleep in the chair. Too stubborn for his own good."

"That sounds like my daughter." He looked around. "It was so quiet I thought I was the only one still up."

"No." She folded her arms over her chest. "But why are you?"

"I have to put out the presents from Santa."

"Right. And the big guy is supposed to get milk and cookies." She glanced at the empty coffee table.

"Damn." He dragged his fingers through his hair. "I forgot about that."

"Uh-oh. Your daughter would have something to say. And this isn't your first rodeo. You can't even claim it's a rookie move." She figured he probably had a lot on his mind.

"Yeah." His expression was adorably sheepish. "I'm not sure what happened but I can give you the perfect storm of excuses. The first Christmas in Montana. Big dinner at Dad's. A military guest of honor. And Wren didn't remind me."

"Still, Hunter—" She teased him with a pitying look. "Epic dad fail."

"Yeah, I know."

"Waking her up is not a good move, so plan B. Take before and after pictures. Full plate, then cookies with bites out of them.

Drink half the milk. Show her Santa was here. She'll believe."

"Good idea. And you're right about not waking her. It will have to do," he said.

"Trust me. With hours of therapy she'll be fine."

His mouth curved up slightly at the corners. "I feel much better now. No guilt at all."

"Happy to help." For a few moments she'd managed to forget she would be gone soon and then the sadness of that fact was back. But for right now she was still his employee. "Do you want a hand putting out her Santa presents?"

He hesitated a moment, then said, "Yeah. I'd appreciate it."

Together they made several trips up and down the stairs, carrying gifts wrapped in paper and ribbon that Wren hadn't seen. They'd been hidden in his closet. Merry knelt under the tree to arrange them. In spite of her heavy heart she was glad she would still be here to see the happy look on that little girl's face tomorrow morning when she would first see this pile of presents. At least Wren would have a carefree Christmas. The following day it would be time to break the news that Merry was leaving.

She looked at Hunter. "I'll help you put that snack out for Santa."

"Right." He held out his hand to help her up.

She wanted to touch him, partly because it might be the last time. She put her fingers into his palm and savored the warmth of his big hand around hers. But dwelling on that was going to make her cry.

After he pulled her to her feet, she quickly broke the contact, then walked into the kitchen and got a Christmas-themed paper plate. After opening a tin of homemade cookies, she asked, "How many of these can Santa eat?"

"Two and a half."

"So, three it is." She set them on the plate then poured milk into a glass tumbler. "Okay, I'll set this on the coffee table."

"Wait." He went to the refrigerator and opened it. "Just one more thing."

"Santa, what a big appetite you have."

"It's not for me." He reached into one of the crisper drawers and pulled out a carrot, then held it up. "This is for the reindeer."

"What?" She'd just been remembering the Santa snack from when she was a little girl. Who did this besides her father? Merry felt tingles from head to toe. "Why?"

"I'm a rancher. I feed the livestock. Horses have to eat frequently because they're big animals. So are reindeer." He held up the raw carrot again. "Bon appétit, Rudolph."

"It's a sign," she whispered.

"I'm sorry?"

She would bet everything she owned that her father, wherever he was, approved of this man and was encouraging her to not give up without a fight. "Hunter, we need to talk."

"About?"

"The elephant in the room," she said.

He looked puzzled but said, "We're going to need a lot more carrots."

"I'm serious. Ever since the night of Wren's play you've been acting weird." Merry could almost see his guard coming up and emotion shutting down. This time she was having none of it. She'd faced the worst-case scenario and could live with the consequences. There was nothing more to lose. It *would* hurt more if she let him go without trying. "I'm not imagining this. You started acting weird right after Wren talked about it being the best night ever because she had a dad and mom, like all the other kids."

"Merry, I don't know—"

"In case you aren't already aware of this, I love Wren very much. She makes that very easy. And I'm so happy to be in her life, hopefully making a positive difference. But I'm not trying to take her mother's place. There's no way I could do that."

"I know." He reached a hand out then lowered it to his side without touching her. "I know you're not."

"Then just answer one question. It doesn't matter what you say as long as you tell me the truth. I can deal with it either way." She took a deep breath then asked, "Are you still in love with your wife?"

The direct question seemed to take him by surprise and he didn't say anything right away. He was thoughtful for several moments, then sighed. "I loved Lara very much and I always will. But I'm not in love with her now."

"You sound very sure of that." There was a flutter in her chest and she was pretty sure that was hope stirring to life. "Are you?"

"Very."

"How can you be?"

"Because I'm in love with you," he said simply.

For a second, happiness exploded inside her, given that the words were everything she wanted to hear. Then the glow faded and pesky reality sneaked in before she could shut it out. She still had questions.

"If you love me, why are you pushing me away?"

He looked lost and his eyes were grim.

"The only explanation I have is that I'm messed up." He spread his hands in a help-less gesture.

"I appreciate your honesty." She truly meant that. It was something at least after trying to guess what he was thinking, why his mood changed so suddenly. "And it makes sense. You've been through a lot."

He nodded. "It's just that I'm having a hard time putting myself in a position where I could go through it again. And protecting Wren is the most important thing—"

"She could get hurt, too."

"Yeah," he whispered.

Merry saw the conflict raging in him and longed to offer comfort. She had to touch him and pressed her body to his, putting her arms around him before resting her cheek against his chest. His heart was hammering. *Proof of life*, she thought, *and it should be lived*. After losing her father, she was more convinced of that than ever. And Hunter had so much love to give.

"I can't give you a guarantee that the future will be perfect, but with a great deal of certainty I can say that it won't even be close to that if you don't take a chance."

"Merry—"

"I'm not finished. And you don't have to say anything, but I need you to hear this." She moved away from him, just far enough to see his face, the look in his eyes. "You are one of the best men I've ever known. I'm not going anywhere. And I promise that I will wait for you to figure things out. As long as it takes. Because that's the way I love."

He nodded but there was no peace in his expression. Without a word he moved away from her then grabbed his sheepskin jacket hanging on the hook beside the door. And then he walked out. He was just gone.

Merry desperately wanted another mistle-snow wish. This was a bad time to realize that giving him the okay to say nothing was without a doubt her most boneheaded move. Looking at the plate of cookies with a side of carrot, she smiled sadly.

"I didn't win, but at least I fought for him, Daddy."

If only her father was there to hold her while she cried.

"Wake up! It's Christmas."

Merry opened her eyes and it wasn't easy. The sun was barely up. And wait. Didn't she just fall asleep five minutes ago? Sleep was hard to come by when the man you loved walked out. Come to think of it, she'd been awake for hours after that and didn't hear him come back.

She sat up and looked at Wren standing by the bed. "Is your dad awake, sweetie?"

"He's not in his room. I checked. And I'm not s'posed to go downstairs by myself and see if Santa came yet."

"Maybe your dad is feeding the animals. I'll throw on some clothes and go find him."

"I wanna go with you."

"Okay. Get dressed." She put on a brave face along with jeans, boots and a sweater, but this situation was not good. Everything

Hunter did was about being a devoted dad. No way he wouldn't be here when his daughter woke up on Christmas morning. Unless something was wrong.

Merry steered the little girl out the back door to keep the "Santa surprises" a secret until, hopefully, her father could be here to see her reaction. His truck was gone but he might have been hauling hay for the animals or using it for any of a hundred other ranch chores that had to be done even on holidays. It wasn't by the barn either, but they still checked the stalls and tack room without success.

"Where could he be?" Wren asked.

"He must have had an errand." It was the hardest thing she'd ever done, but Merry managed to keep her voice neutral and calm when she felt just the opposite.

"But I wanna open presents. I've been waitin' so long."

"I know, sweetie. It must be an important errand."

Or something bad had happened. Something that needed the sheriff involved. With every step back to the house it was harder to hold off the panic and Merry didn't know what to do.

When they walked back into the kitchen, Jack was there. He was dressed in jeans and a flannel shirt but his hair was sticking up and there was a shadow of stubble on his face. But he'd never looked better to her. She wasn't alone.

"Merry Christmas." There were questions in his eyes. "When I woke up to an empty house, I thought this was a *Twilight Zone* holiday."

"Sorry." She looked down at the little girl pressed tightly against her, then rubbed a hand reassuringly down Wren's arm. "We went to see if Hunter was in the barn."

Jack nodded slightly, letting her know he got her concern and wouldn't say anything alarming. "What does a guy have to do to get a cup of coffee around here?"

"Push a button." The water and grounds were ready to go in the coffee maker. It's one of the things she'd done when sleep wouldn't come last night. "Wren, why don't you show him how it's done?"

"Over here, Uncle Jack."

His eyebrows went up, an indication that he didn't miss his elevation in rank. "I'm right behind you, squirt."

That's what he used to call her, Merry thought.

Although Wren loved to do it, she magnanimously allowed her new uncle to do the button-pushing honors. Moments later the sound of water dripping into the pot filled the kitchen, followed quickly by the rich aroma of brewing coffee. Normally Merry loved it but her stomach was in knots and she was afraid she was going to throw up. Every second that ticked by without a word from Hunter was like a shot of adrenaline to her nerves.

She looked at Jack. If Hunter was at the main house he would have walked so his truck would still be there. And it wasn't. He'd gone somewhere and hadn't returned.

"I'm wondering if I should call the *S-H-E-R-I-F-F*."

"Sheriff?" Wren's eyes went wide.

"I forgot how smart you are." Some teacher she was going to be, Merry thought. And a crisis management failure on top of it. She tried to smile at the little girl and hoped somehow it was reassuring. "I'm sure everything is fine and—"

The sound of the front door opening interrupted her. Then a deep voice calling out, "Ho, ho, ho. Merry Christmas!"

"Daddy!"

The little girl raced out of the room and Merry was right behind her. Jack brought up the rear and the three of them came to a dead stop when they saw Hunter. He was wearing his ever-present Stetson but on top of that was a deluxe Santa hat with faux white fur trim and a matching pompom. His arms were full of wrapped presents that he'd just carried inside.

"It's a beautiful day." He put everything

under the tree, then said to Jack, "There's more in the truck. Mind giving me a hand?"

"Happy to."

The two men brought everything inside and set the presents by the tree. It looked like Christmas exploded in the cabin's front room.

Wren hugged her father. "We couldn't find you, Daddy. Merry was gonna call the sheriff. She spelled it but I knew anyway."

Hunter picked her up. "I'm sorry you were worried. I had some last-minute shopping to do."

"All night?" Merry asked.

"In Kalispell a few stores were open all night. But there was this one—" He smiled mysteriously. "It took a little longer than I expected."

Wren's arms were around his neck. "Can we open presents now? Santa came and I don't think I can wait much longer."

"Let's do it." He squeezed her tight for a moment, then set her down.

It was a paper-ripping, gift-opening free-for-all that seemed to go on forever. Wren was giddy with excitement when she saw her new princess doll with its royal wardrobe. Other packages revealed socks, pajamas, mittens, a scarf, a scooter and a sparkly pink helmet.

Hunter handed Jack a box. "You look like a Scotch drinker. It's not imaginative, but next year I'll do better."

Jack's eyes narrowed for a moment, then he nodded his understanding. "Later I'll open it and we'll drink to next year."

Merry heard that exchange and added another question to the list she had for Hunter. Right now she was keeping busy shoving used wrapping paper into a trash bag. Finally all the packages had been opened and the contents neatly stacked under the tree.

"It looks like that's a wrap. Pun intended," she said.

"Merry, look." Wren pointed to a tall present sitting alone by the front door. "There's one more."

Hunter grabbed it before his daughter could. "That's not for you, kiddo."

"Who then?" she asked.

"Merry." There was an expression in his eyes that had never been there before. He set it down in front of her. "Merry Christmas."

"Hunter, I—"

"Just open it, please."

"Okay." It was tall but she had to get on her knees because her legs were shaking. Her hands were shaking, too, as she carefully unwrapped the beautiful gold foil paper to reveal a plain box. She lifted the flaps and found another wrapped box inside. Puzzled, she met his gaze. "What—"

Emotions scrolled across his face too quickly to identify. "Keep going."

She nodded, then lifted out the gift and slid the paper off, only to find yet another box. This happened three more times and her excitement and anticipation grew even as the boxes got smaller. Especially because they got smaller. Finally, there was one left and she found a black velvet jewelry box inside.

"Hunter?"

"There weren't any jewelry stores open twenty-four hours on Christmas Eve. But when you have enough money and determination, doors open for you."

"So this is what took you so long?"

"Yes."

"Merry said you must be doing something important," Wren said.

"I definitely was." He smiled down at her before moving in front of Merry. He took the box from her palm then helped her to her feet.

"What are you doing?"

Without answering, he went down on one knee and opened the box, revealing a stunning vintage diamond engagement ring. He looked at her expectantly. "Will you marry me?"

Her heart was hammering so hard she wasn't sure she could speak. That was incredibly inconvenient at the most important moment of her life. The love for him that she'd kept bottled up inside was straining to be set free. But she had to know something first.

"Does this mean you figured things out? That you're not afraid anymore?"

"Oh, I'm terrified." But he didn't look it. Hope sparkled in his eyes where once there'd only been emptiness. "The only thing that scared me more than taking this step was not taking it."

"So, you figured things out pretty fast."

"As soon as I walked out the door last night," he agreed. "I'm in love with you and will always be afraid of losing you. But I won't let it be because I gave up on us without trying."

Merry stared at him for several moments, too stunned to speak. Her brother, on the other hand, had no problem at all.

"For crying out loud, sis, will you put the man out of his misery and say yes already?"

Hunter nodded at him. "I'd have asked your permission the old-fashioned way, but due to my own stupidity and the necessity of a big gesture to cancel it out, the timeline had to be altered."

"Understood," Jack said. "Permission granted."

And Wren, who'd been uncharacteristically silent through all this, said, "Are you going to marry Daddy? Can I be a flower girl? And wear a tiara?"

"I'd say she approves." Merry smiled at him.

"So is that a yes?" Hunter asked. "I want it to be. But only if it's what you want, too. I don't want to push—"

"Yes." She held out her left hand for him to slide the ring on. When he did, she sighed at the exquisite diamond and the perfect fit, then tugged him to his feet. "I want this more than I can say. It's what I wished for on that very first mistlesnow."

"See? I told you mistlesnow wishes worked," Wren said happily. "And I told you this was going to be the best Christmas ever."

"You were right," Merry and Hunter said together.

And then he kissed her. No mistletoe required.

Epilogue

Hunter held tightly to Merry's hand as they walked to his father's place. Wren had run ahead with Jack right behind her. Walking beside the woman he loved so much made him happy and he planned to do it for the rest of his life. The darkness he'd carried inside him for so long didn't stand a chance against a woman named Merry.

"I can't wait to tell everyone our good news," he said. "How do you feel about a short engagement?"

She leaned her head against his shoulder. "That works for me. Maybe we should go to

Rustler's Notch for a destination wedding. Max would like that."

"I'm more interested in what you want." He looked down at her, golden hair framing her face like a halo. An angel. And she was his.

"As long as the whole family is there, we can get married in the barn for all I care." Smiling, she met his gaze. "We'll talk to Jack and see how long the military can spare him. I feel as if I have my brother back and I want him to walk me down the aisle."

"Sounds like a plan."

They were almost at his father's, and in front of the two-story log cabin it looked like a car lot with all the vehicles lined up. There was a decorated tree in the window with white lights twinkling. On the front porch they smiled at each other, then took a deep breath.

"Here we go," he said. "Are you ready?"

"Are you?" she teased.

"More than you can possibly know."

Hunter didn't bother knocking. Family

never did. He opened the door and walked into Crawford central, where everyone was talking excitedly. Wren was with her aunts and Jack was shaking hands with Max. Introductions had apparently been made. Someone, probably Lily, had been cooking because mouthwatering smells were coming from the kitchen.

"Hello, everyone." Hunter let go of Merry's hand long enough to wave a greeting. "Merry Christmas."

The whole crew stopped their conversations and welcomed them.

Wilder said to their father, "Everyone is here. Can we eat now?"

"Don't ask me. That's up to our chef. Lily?"

"It's all ready. But I could use extra hands to put everything out on the table."

"Oh, let me help," Merry said. "I feel like such a slacker for not pitching in."

"No worries." Lily's green eyes sparkled with more than Christmas spirit. "You've had a lot going on today. What with your brother visiting," she added.

Everyone rallied around and brought out mashed potatoes, freshly baked biscuits, various side dishes that were enough to feed an army and a standing rib roast. The seating went pretty much like Thanksgiving with Logan and Sarah on one side of a high chair for Sophia and Hunter's daughter on the other. Seeing Wren with her baby cousin reminded Hunter of their earlier conversation. After his proposal, Wren had asked for a baby sister and Merry had given the child a hard yes on that. She loved children and was going to be a teacher, after all. He would be nervous for nine months but he'd deal with it. And something told him it would turn out all right.

After much juggling and repositioning, everyone was finally settled and Hunter wanted to make his announcement while there was still a shred of sanity in the room. He tapped his fork against the water glass by his plate, demanding their attention.

"Before we start, I have something to say." He smiled at the amazing woman beside him. "I proposed to Merry and she said yes. We're getting married."

Hunter was prepared for everyone to start talking at once. He anticipated hearing congratulations, good-natured teasing and sincere wishes for a lifetime of happiness. And from Max he figured there would be some taking credit for the match because he'd suggested hiring a nanny for that wedding weekend. None of that happened. There was total silence.

Baffled, Hunter looked around the table. "Who are you people and what have you done with my family?"

They all looked at each other then burst out laughing.

"Gotcha," Logan said.

"Do you really think we didn't know?" Genevieve looked at her husband and Knox gave him an I-told-you-so smirk.

"There were so many clues to pick from." Finn took Avery's hand and she smiled at him. "You couldn't stop touching each other."

"Not to mention that ring," Lily chimed in. "That rock is so big and shiny I think it's visible from space."

Merry held up her hand to give them all a better look. "It is beautiful, isn't it? Hunter has very good taste. I'm a lucky woman."

"And he's a lucky man." Max wore an expression of fatherly pride on his face, but there was something else, too. It was the unmistakable satisfaction of a conspiracy. "But if there was any doubt about this engagement, your daughter took care of that when she spilled the beans as soon as she ran into the house."

"I didn't spill anything, Gramps." Taking the remark literally produced an expression of self-righteous indignation that his little girl had perfected. "I just said that Daddy was going to marry Merry. I get to be in the wedding and she's going to be my mom."

Those words didn't produce complete silence. There were some sniffles around the table, and not just from the women.

"Oh, hell," Wilder blurted.

"Language," Hunter reminded him.

"Sorry. But I just thought of something." He glanced around the table at all the couples and got only blank stares. "This means my brothers have all deserted me. I'm the last Crawford bachelor."

Max chuckled. "Don't look now, son, but I'm right there with you."

If anything, Wilder's tragic expression deepened. "Says the man paying to get us all married off. That doesn't make me feel any better, Dad."

"Suck it up, kid," Finn told him. Then he looked at Hunter and Merry. "You two will be the next Crawford couple to take on the mysterious diary."

"Oh—" Merry looked at Hunter. "What with everything going on I forgot to tell you. The night of Wren's play I found out something—"

There was a knock at the door, as loud and startling as a gunshot. Hunter wondered who it could be. The whole family was here and none of them would knock anyway. He and

Wilder were closest and both of them stood at the same time.

With Max right behind them, they hurried to find out who was there. Hunter opened the door and heard the sound of a car driving away. Then he looked down and what he saw shocked him to the core. It was an infant car seat with a sleeping baby inside. There was a note pinned to a blue blanket.

Wilder, this is your baby. I've done the best I could for four months and I can't do it anymore. A boy needs a dad and you're Cody's, so it's your turn now. Please take good care of him.
L

Hunter looked at his brother and felt shock and a little bit of satisfaction. Wilder was the one who'd wanted Hunter to be his wingman at their brother's wedding and help him hit on women. The same man who'd advised him to let off some steam even though he had a six-year-old daughter to take care of.

"Well, little brother, looks like you got a

baby for Christmas." He didn't know if this was karma or payback but either was a bitch. "Loosen up. You're going to have to be a dirty diaper–changing kind of guy after all."

* * * * *

LET'S TALK

Romance

For exclusive extracts, competitions and special offers, find us online:

f facebook.com/millsandboon

⊙ @millsandboonuk

𝕐 @millsandboon

Or get in touch on 0844 844 1351*

For all the latest titles coming soon, visit millsandboon.co.uk/nextmonth

Want even more
ROMANCE?

Join our bookclub today!

'Mills & Boon books, the perfect way to escape for an hour or so.'

Miss W. Dyer

'Excellent service, promptly delivered and very good subscription choices.'

Miss A. Pearson

'You get fantastic special offers and the chance to get books before they hit the shops'

Mrs V. Hall

Visit millsandbook.co.uk/Bookclub and save on brand new books.

MILLS & BOON